The

Promise

For my Rory.

You taught me how strong I could be. I will never stop

fighting for you my darling.

The Gratitude Page

This book would not have been possible without the support of some very special people.

Firstly, to my husband. For keeping the children out of the room while I wrote, for bringing me food and beverages, thus ensuring my survival and the completion of the book, and for your technical wizardry. Also, for not divorcing me during my manic mood-swings in those hectic few weeks before the book launch. And for your Aramis hair. Just because. You are incredible, thank you.

To my wonderful friend and fellow author, JL Morse. For your skills as an honest, constructive, yet very flattering beta reader. For pointing out the questions I had left unanswered and giving me confidence to share this story with the world. Thank you.

To my team of advanced readers, who gave me wonderful and very helpful feedback and several of whom helped me to choose the book cover design and narrow down my vision. You have no idea how much I rely on you all, thank you so very much.

To you, my beautiful readers. This story was a

form of therapy for me to write, and it means the world to me that you would choose to add it to your collection. Many of you have followed me from my non-fiction, natural parenting writing and I am so happy that you've continued to be so supportive of my work. Wherever and however you found your way here, I'm glad you did. Thank you so much.

And lastly, and quite possibly most importantly, to my two beautiful, brave, playful and often challenging little children. My inspiration in all that I do. My motivation. My muses. Without you there would be no stories. Thank you my angels.

Not flesh of my flesh, nor bone of my bone, but still miraculously my own.
Never forget for a single minute, you didn't grow under my heart, but in it.

Fleur Conkling Heyliger

Chapter One

Emily leaned over the tiny stainless steel sink, pulling her long black hair to one side and holding it in place as she bent forward to wash her face. The water splashed down onto the dark haired baby she wore strapped to her chest, and he squealed nuzzling his cheek into her cardigan, rubbing the moisture away. She winced as the icy water turned her fingertips blue, and reached over to the soap dispenser only to find it empty. Again.

Sighing, Emily took a handful of paper towels and rubbed the rough surface over her skin until she was dry. She took one more and held it under the trickling tap, then squeezed it in her fingers, watching the excess water filter away. She leaned forward, dangling the baby backwards so that she could reach his face, and deftly used the damp paper to clean his skin.

He arched away and she grinned, dipping into the woven wrap, locating a sticky hand and pulling it free. She cleaned it thoroughly and then found the other one. "No need to look so worried, Flynn," she muttered. "It's way to cold for a big wash, you're getting away with the bare minimum today, lucky boy!"

Balling the damp paper towels in her palm, she tossed them into the bin then grabbed her backpack, slinging the heavy weight onto her shoulders. Loud, happy voices echoed through the public toilets, and Emily looked behind her to see two women entering, one blonde and soft looking, one pixie like redhead, both pushing buggies overladen with changing bags and souvenirs. Emily immediately spotted a plastic bag with the Natural History Museum logo on it and smiled widely. Jackpot.

Without a doubt, the best thing about being homeless in London was the tourists. They never failed to surprise her with their sheer naivety. Stealing from them, conning them in some way or another, it was almost too simple. But Emily didn't crave challenge, she didn't wish they would make it a little harder to get what she wanted. What she craved was food. Money to buy clothes for her growing son, safety. Day to day life was challenging enough. The easy tourists were a gift and she hoped these two wouldn't let her down.

Emily smiled confidently at them and pushed her numerous fake gold and silver bangles up her forearm, pointing to the two sleeping toddlers in their buggies. "Long day?" she asked.

"Yes," the blonde woman sighed happily. "We've seen everything. They've had so much fun!"

"How old are they?"

"Both two. This is Thomas," she said, pointing to the red cheeked, blonde haired boy in front of her. "And this is Elizabeth," she gestured to her friend's child. "How old is yours?"

Emily looked down at her son, smiling with pride. "He's ten months."

"You're not wearing any shoes," the pixie woman exclaimed, noticing the dirty bare feet poking out from beneath her flowing skirt. "Is this a new fashion thing? You must be freezing!"

"Uh, no, not a fashion thing," Emily replied, swinging her long skirt forward to cover the pale, mottled skin of her numb feet. "More a stepped in a big puddle thing. They're in my bag. I was just going to go and get some new ones for the journey home," she lied, not wanting to tell them the truth. That she had swapped her shoes last week for a BLT and a Starbucks latte with "Woozy Susie." It had been getting dark and Emily hadn't eaten all day, when Susie, a no nonsense, afro haired, pickled livered, sixty year old woman who had been on the streets most her life, had struck up the deal with her. She had been too hungry to even think of saying no.

For some reason, and she couldn't fathom why, she got a lot less charity than others in the area. It was a constant source of surprise to her. She had thought that being a mother and quite obviously struggling to feed and clothe her baby, people would be falling over themselves to help her, but it wasn't like that. If anything, they judged her harder and ignored her even more than the standard prescription for the misfortunate. If only they knew what she had been through to end up in this situation. If only they would open their minds for a second and give her a chance to explain. But they never did. They just hurried by, busy with their own lives, their own worries.

So, she had no shoes. In October. In London. But she *did* have a pair of thick woollen socks. She just wasn't about to ruin them walking around the streets in the filth and wet all day, when she could save them and have warm, dry feet tonight.

"I see," the red head said uneasily, breaking eye contact. Emily smiled warmly, and looked away. Her goal was to look wholesome and trustworthy, not an easy thing to accomplish when she was waiting for an opportunity to prove them wrong, but she had been around long enough to know how to play the game. Hell, even before her street life she'd had to hone her skills as an actress.

Pretending. Lying. Trying to keep *him* from seeing the truth, to keep herself safe from his volatile mood swings. She shuddered, not surprised by the sudden turn of her thoughts. She regularly had flashbacks and nightmares, and she thought she saw him at least twice a week. She would be walking along the street and there he would be, striding purposefully towards her. Or sitting opposite her on the platform at the train station. Eating a sandwich outside a café as she queued with her collection of loose change to buy a cup of tea.

When that happened, she would melt into the walls, hide her face and hold her breath. She couldn't risk him finding her, finding Flynn. It always took her hours to resume her sense of normality after these false sightings.

But right now, she needed to focus. She glanced over at the women. The pixie was taking a tampon out of her bag, the blonde busily peeling back the blanket from the hot, sleeping child. She needed them to feel comfortable, to see her as just another mother, not as a potential threat. She turned on the water again, making a show of washing her hands. Stalling. The two women parked their buggies beside the sinks and both of them went into the stalls.

Unbelievable, Emily thought, shaking her head. Though she had seen it time and time again, she still couldn't understand what must be going through their minds. To leave not only their belongings, their valuables, but also their precious children right there for the taking in a dirty, public toilet in the middle of London. Emily instinctively wrapped her arms around Flynn, sick at the thought of what could happen if the wrong person saw the unattended children.

Perhaps, she thought introspectively, her fear was a product of her past. Maybe these women had led such blessed lives that they couldn't fathom a time when their luck would run out and fate would strike them down, leaving them ruined. She hoped they would never have to face the consequences of such trusting naivety.

She waited three seconds, wiping her palms dry on her skirt, then walked straight to where the two toddlers were sleeping, completely unaware of the world around them. With expert fingers, she slid a handful of nappies, a packet of wet wipes and one of the two purses from the open bags. She riffled through the purse and found forty pounds in cash.

Grinning, she slipped the now empty purse back into the bag and without hesitating a second longer, walked straight out of the toilets. Forty pounds! She felt like jumping up and down with excitement. They would be eating tonight. And she might even splash out and buy some shoes if she could find a cheap pair. She made for the back streets, knowing they would never find her, already pushing their faces from her mind.

She never let herself think about the effect her actions would have on the people she targeted. She couldn't. Yes, it was harsh, yes it would be a little crack in their otherwise perfect day, but she never took credit cards or personal things, and she knew they would manage without it. What would be a nice takeaway or a family day out for them, would mean her and Flynn could eat every day for a fortnight or maybe more. She didn't feel bad taking from them. It was necessary.

Emily could feel the eyes burning into her back as she walked the aisles of the busy supermarket, a basket slung over her arm. She had found a pair of trainers only one size too big for four pounds in the sale bin, and she had made straight for the reduced food section, marked down because it only had a few hours of shelf life left. Four sandwiches marked at thirty pence each and a tub of strawberries for ten pence lay alongside the shoes in her basket. She glanced over her shoulder to see the young, burly security guard following closely behind. *This was bullshit*. She had money in her pocket and she knew she hadn't done anything wrong.

Emily hated the way people treated her because she was struggling. Homeless. They were scared of her, wary, and she couldn't stand it. This time two years ago she had been shopping in Waitrose, driving a Fiat, a part of society. She had lost everything in the course of one day, but that didn't change who she was deep down. A good, person. A kind person. But nobody ever saw that, did they? They saw only the stereotype. It wasn't fair.

And though she didn't bat an eye at stealing one on one, she would never take the risk of stealing from a real shop. She wouldn't dare, for fear of being hemmed in by security. Of not being able to get out. Of having them take Flynn from her. She was always on her best behaviour in places like this. So why on earth was he following her?

"Miss?"

She turned, a false smile plastered on her face. "Yes?"

"I'm going to have to ask you to leave, if you could just follow me please," the guard said, reaching forward and forcibly taking her basket from her.

"What? Why?"

"You know your kind aren't allowed in here."

"My kind?" she asked, reeling from his insult.

"You know."

"No, I don't. I haven't a clue what you're on about. I just want to buy my food and I'll be going," she said, reaching to take the basket from him.

"Don't make a scene. Come on, let's go."

"No! What have I done? I'm trying to buy food for my son, I haven't done anything wrong!"

"We have enough of you lot coming in here and taking stuff without paying. This ain't a charity, love. Go to a soup kitchen or somethin', but don't be coming back here. You ain't welcome."

"I'm not homeless, I'm a backpacker. *Fuck*. I didn't

do anything wrong, just let me buy the food and then I'll go. I'm not here to cause trouble, I just want to eat, for gods sake!"

"You ain't got no money, look at you, you don't even have any shoes on and the kids not dressed for this weather," he said, pointing at Flynn's bare feet.

"I'm *buying* shoes, look!" she shouted, pointing at the basket in his meaty hand. "How am I supposed to wear shoes if you won't let me buy them?"

A crowd of curious onlookers was beginning to form at the end of the aisle, though Emily noticed that they kept a safe distance away. Wouldn't want to get too close to the crazy homeless lady now, would they? The security guard glanced at them, frowning, then leaned towards Emily, a menacing expression on his face.

"Do I need to call for assistance or are you gonna get out?"

Emily glared at him venomously, hatred burning in her eyes. It wasn't fair. None of this was fair. Every ounce of her wanted to fight this, to stand up for herself and win. But she couldn't risk it. The police would never take her side, that was just the way it went. With an angry grunt, she let go of the basket, her gaze resting briefly on the food she wouldn't get to eat. The shoes she wouldn't get to wear. "Fine. I'll go somewhere else," she said, her fist clenching tightly around the money in her pocket.

With all the dignity she could muster, she turned and walked away, the sound of the crowd's disapproving mutters ringing in her ears. His heavy footsteps followed behind her all the way to the exit.

Chapter Two

Emily walked as far and as fast from the scene of her humiliation as she could, tears streaming silently down her face. She hated that she had let that arrogant jobsworth get to her. She hated that he had power over her, that she had let him make her feel so desperate.

But she *was* desperate. She couldn't deny it. She would have begged if she thought he would have given in and shown her some humility. She would have shown him the money in her pocket if she hadn't been sure he would take it or call the police on suspicion of theft. Which of course it bloody was. She couldn't have changed his mind about her no matter what she had done. She had learned that the hard way when she'd first come to the streets. Some people will see what they want to see no matter what you try to do to change their minds. There was no point in even trying.

Her feet were ice cold and cut to shreds and she realised with a sigh that she would have to stop. The pain was too much to bear. She stepped off the pavement, into the doorway of an abandoned betting shop. Sinking against the rough concrete wall Emily felt her legs weaken, and she slid down to sit on the cold hard ground. Flynn was rousing and beginning to kick his legs against her stomach, and Emily felt a fresh wave of tears began to fall. She was so drained at the the thought of feeding him again.

Her milk had been suffering lately after a run of bad luck and not enough food, and as a result, her nipples were chapped and sore from Flynn sucking harder than usual, trying desperately to get his fill. It broke her heart to see him so hungry, and she knew he wasn't as big as he could be. But hard as it was, she was thankful to have a way to feed him for free. Some days he was the only one of them who got to eat.

She released him from the woven wrap, letting the soft material land in a pile of rainbow hemp on her lap. Running her fingers over the buttery soft fabric, she thought back to how the beautiful sling had found its way into her possession. She had been nine months pregnant and ready to burst. All she could think about was how she was going to survive once the life inside of her emerged, how she was going to keep her baby from freezing to death.

She had been approached on the street by several volunteers as the months had passed and her belly had swollen, though the rest of her had shrunk considerably. Nice people, trying to help, to make a difference. They wanted her to come with them. Somewhere safe, somewhere she could birth her baby in peace, warm, dry and off the freezing London streets. And she had wanted to.

But her fear of being found was too great. She couldn't bring herself to trust them. The thought of putting her life in the hands of another fallible human being was too big a step for her to take. As she had stood outside the women's refuge, feeling the slow tumbles and turns of her child within her womb, she knew the risk was too great. She could never give herself over to these strangers, not when she was at her weakest. Not when she would be too consumed with birthing her baby to defend herself.

Devastated by the chance she couldn't take, the

warmth she had to refuse, she had turned and walked away, tears blinding her vision as she pictured her naked baby, blue and shivering in her arms. She *had* to do something. She had to provide for her child. Starving and exhausted, she had trawled the city for hours until she'd spotted what she was looking for. A group of mothers, chatting and laughing, their babies wrapped up warm in prams and pushchairs. One mother wore her daughter close to her body, the colourful material layered over and over her, creating the cosiest of nests. Emily could not take her eyes from the woman.

She had followed them blindly, stepping over the threshold of a building without registering its name. A woman in a purple t-shirt had approached her and introduced herself. "I'm Sarah, welcome to La Leche League. Is this your first baby?" she'd asked, gesturing to the enormous bump Emily was unconsciously rubbing. Emily had nodded in confusion. "And you want to learn more about breastfeeding? That's great!" Sarah said, without waiting for an answer. "We'll get started in a minute, it's just through here," she indicated the door behind her.

"Can I use the toilet first?" Emily asked.

"Of course, it's right there. I'll save you a seat," Sarah replied, disappearing through the double doors with a cheery smile. Emily had looked around to find herself in a wide entrance hall, buggies and prams lined up along the wall. The mothers had all disappeared into the room already.

And there, lying casually over one of the icandy pushchairs, had been the beautiful woven sling. Emily had paused only for a second. Then she'd taken everything. Three changing bags stuffed full of nappies, clothes and blankets. She had emptied the cash from the purses, and taken all the food she could find. And lastly, she had picked up the precious woven wrap, stuffing it haphazardly into one of the bags. And she had left, riddled with guilt, yet utterly relieved.

The sling had been the hardest to take. She'd wanted it more than anything, but hated that the other mother had to lose it. She had worn it like it was a part of her body, radiating absolute joy at her closeness to her child. Emily had wanted to *be* her in that moment, wanted to walk right into her body and take her place. Envious wasn't strong enough to describe how she had felt watching her, admiring her. But she hadn't regretted it.

That night her waters had broken. She had been able to clean her newborn son and put him in a dry nappy. She had dressed him warmly in layers of soft, clean cotton and wrapped him against her chest, sharing her body heat with him. She had not regretted it.

She smoothed the fabric over her lap now, and repositioned the baby. He squealed impatiently and she brought him to her breast, where he suckled ravenously. Her own stomach growled and she felt sick and hot, though the air was cool. She *had to* eat. If the supermarket wouldn't let her buy food, there were plenty of places that would.

She thought of where to go. Looking up, she realised she was only two streets down from Bunny's fish and chip shop. Just the thought of the heavy food in her stomach, imagining the smell of grease and batter was enough to make her salivate. Silently, she willed Flynn to finish his feed so she could move on. It seemed to take an age, and she was sure from the fussing and squealing he was making that he wasn't getting enough. She was losing too much weight. *Chips.* That was the answer. Definitely chips.

She eased him back into the wrap, ignoring his protests and holding a finger to his lips for him to suck on in the absence of a breast. He silenced and busied himself with chewing painfully on her knuckle. She barely noticed. Her legs swayed as she pulled herself up to her feet and she looked ahead, suddenly remembering the alleyway that cut through the roads creating a short-cut.

With a wry smile she made for it, walking down the narrow pathway between two tall buildings, her thoughts entirely focused on her need for food. There was nothing that stood between her and her dinner. Nothing going to take priority over her filling her stomach.

Perhaps it was this single minded determination that distracted her from her usually vigilant awareness.

But as she felt herself falling forwards, she only just had time to brace her hands on the ground, her arms forming a protective cage around the baby on her chest. The back of her head throbbed and she could smell the metallic tang of blood. *Her* blood. She looked over her shoulder, feeling dizzy, wondering in bewilderment what had hit her so hard.

The figure loomed over her, and Emily felt a wave of utter panic as she tried to focus on his dark features. *Was it him?* "Karl?" she murmured, rubbing her grazed palm over her eyes as she strained to look at the man towering above. His face came into focus. *It wasn't him.* She felt a giddy sense of relief that was unfitting for the situation. *It wasn't him.*

"What av' you got?" he slurred, his eyes unfocused yet strangely piercing all at once. The sense of relief left her immediately, fear gripping her tightly in its place.

"Wh... what?" she stuttered, pushing herself backwards, out of his reach. She dragged herself to her feet, only to feel his hands clamp tightly around her throat. She tried to speak, to plead for Flynn's sake, but she couldn't make a sound. As quickly as he had seized her, he released her and she bent forward, gasping for air, one arm wrapping tightly around her baby.

She watched him, wondering if she could run, if he was drunk or high. He spun away from her, punching a fist in the air then turned back to face her, his eyes cold and blank. With a filthy hand, he smacked himself across the cheek and screeched, "You see that? Do ya!" Emily nodded, terrified. He was mad, completely deranged.

"So, what av' ya got then?" he screamed, droplets of acrid saliva hitting her in the face.

"What... what do you mean? Drugs? I don't have any!"

"No drugs! No drugs!" he shouted at the sky with a manic laugh. He circled her and she backed against the wall. She had a knife in the top of her bag, but she couldn't reach it without him seeing.

"No," she said with an nervous smile, "No drugs. Sorry." He laughed again and turned away from her. *This* was her chance and she knew she had to take it.

With slow, measured steps, she began to walk backwards down the alley, holding her breath, her eyes focused intently on him.

Without warning, he spun and smiled at her, his broken, yellowed teeth barred. "Money then!" he shouted. "Give me your money!" He didn't wait for an answer. To Emily's horror, he launched himself forward at full speed, running straight at her.

She turned sideways just in the nick of time. His body slammed into hers, throwing her hard into the wall. Flynn bellowed and Emily wanted desperately to sooth him, to check him for injury. But she couldn't right now.

"Gimmie the money!" he shouted. Emily reached a trembling hand into her pocket, grabbing the precious notes and without pausing to think, threw them onto the ground behind him. His eyes glinted wickedly, holding her gaze for an age, a dangerous sneer on his lips. And then, finally he turned from her, walking towards the cash.

Emily didn't hesitate. She turned and ran, ignoring the stinging flesh as her bare feet pounded against the rough, hard ground, blinking against the pain from her wounded head. She ran and she didn't look back.

Chapter Three

Friday evening, Kings Cross station

Saraya Matthews was on autopilot. For six, or perhaps it was seven years, she had made this same daily commute. Today was no different. She nodded to Kev the newsagent from whom she bought chewing gum and the latest tabloids and celeb mags twice a week. Magazines which she had actually stopped reading more than two years ago, disenchanted by the same old stories spiced up with occasionally new faces.

She had caught herself mindlessly flicking through the glossy pages on her lunch break, her eyes glazing over as she read about the latest five hundred calorie celebrity "cleanse" – crash diet – and how *this* singer was getting too fat and *this* actress was cheating, and had finally had an epiphany. She had shut the magazine and immediately felt her shoulders lift.

Now she took a book to read on her lunch break. But she still bought the tabloids. Habit perhaps was the reason, or pity for Kev who was struggling to make ends meet. Who knew? Twice a week she handed over a ten pound note and got a pile of worthless, unchanging drivel which she proceeded to hand over to the vultures in the office.

Saraya was a creature of habit, yet it wasn't through choice but rather a severe lack of it. Her weekends were planned in great detail. A stilted and entirely unenjoyable lunch at her parents' house the first Sunday of every month, which always left her feeling drained for days afterwards. Hairdressers the second Saturday. Evening yoga and mindfulness classes every Saturday at eight p.m and a five mile run like clockwork every Sunday morning. It wasn't that she especially wanted to fill her free time so fully, nor that she was particularly enamoured with fitness. It was simply the fact that without these seemingly important tasks written in ink on her calendar, life was incredibly empty.

Time was a killer. She had once before tried to let go of her "commitments" and be spontaneous for the weekend. Her yoga lesson had been cancelled and her parents had gone to Norfolk for their anniversary, so it was more thrust on her rather than a conscious choice. Everyone else had been busy at such short notice and she had found herself at a loss. Forty-eight hours of silence. Daytime TV, movies in bed, walks round the park. It should have been nice. Relaxing. It wasn't as if she was afraid of her own company. But that two days had been torture.

The clock ticking away each second of wasted time, minutes where she felt that a healthy young woman such as herself, a woman with the world at her feet, should have a million exciting, adventurous or even just productive things she could be doing. Yet she couldn't think of a single one. She had gone into work that Monday morning earlier than ever before, relieved by the knowledge that soon she would have another person to talk to, even if it was only Mandy the cleaner.

But as much as her iron clad routine was saving her, masking her loneliness with busy-work and small talk, lately she had found herself resenting it more and more. As she made her way back home for the fifth time that week, she was lost in thought. This couldn't be it. She couldn't go on like this indefinitely, could she?

A commotion tore her attention towards the ticket barriers, where a man with a shaved head and a tattoo of a green moth on the back of his neck was shouting at the machine, hitting it hard with his fist as his ticket was repeatedly spat out at him. The squat security guard nearby was clearly weighing up whether to stop his conversation with the twenty-something blonde tourist to come over and intervene. His hesitation cost him.

The moth man made a split second decision and leapt the barrier and with a cry of anger, the security guard made a reluctant chase. Saraya watched them go, betting on the moth man. She rolled her eyes. Same shit, different day.

There was something special about Kings Cross station. When she had first moved to London, she had taken her time getting to work, pausing after her journey from leafy Ealing, to take the time to admire the building and watch the people passing through it.

She had loved sitting on a bench with a hot coffee, wondering where everyone was going or coming from, trying to imagine their story. It had been a long time since she had sat and enjoyed a coffee, watching the world go by. Now she just wanted to get to work so she could get it over with and go back home, eat, bath, sleep and do it all again the next day. She was aware that she had traded imagination for irritation. Rushing down the stairs and onto the platform, she made it just in time to see her train arriving.

Saraya elbowed her way through the swarm of hot bodies, all surging forward in a desperate attempt to secure a much coveted seat on the sweltering rush hour tube. She felt the skin of her bare arm graze the foul, sticky armpit of a portly middle aged man dressed inexplicably in a muscle vest, exposing a field of curly wet body hair. Saraya shuddered and moved back a step, only to be rapped sharply on the ankle by an elderly lady with a cane and a surprisingly strong arm.

She fixed the crone with a death stare perfected over years of stressful commuting and smiled victoriously as the woman bowed her head in ungracious apology. Rather than seize the advantage though, Saraya paused, observing her frail old body and shaking hands, the way she swayed ever so slightly as she settled her weight against the cane. Wearily, she stepped aside allowing the wench to take the seat she'd had her eye on. With a sigh, she settled for squeezing herself between the fingerprinted plexiglass and a businessman wearing too much cheap aftershave.

Why, she wondered, was she still having to endure this daily torment? How on earth had she not, at the grand old age of thirty two, managed to get off this miserable merry-go-round and found something more meaningful to do with her life?

As she held her breath trying to avoid the pungent aroma of the man beside her, she evaluated all that she had achieved in her time on this planet. An office job packed with nonsense paperwork, the kind that is devised with the express purpose of filling the time of the worker bees to make them forget they are living an endless ground-hog day of pointless tasks and meaningless goals.

A cursory relationship with her parents. One very bossy, very tedious big sister, who she saw only when she couldn't think up a plausible excuse quickly enough. A handful of friends who, as much as she hated to admit it to herself, she probably wouldn't miss if they suddenly evaporated from her life. And a boyfriend.

A boyfriend. At thirty two years old that just sounded silly to Saraya. She should have a *husband,* or at the very least, a *partner.* But no. She had a boyfriend. And not a particularly special one at that. Admittedly, he was fairly kind and occasionally funny, but she knew that there was something big missing. There was no real connection. No spark. Her heart didn't beat faster when she saw him and when he called off their dates, she breathed a sigh of relief that she didn't have to bother getting dressed up, happily sinking into a deep, hot bath with a good book and a glass of red instead.

In fact, it was this boyfriend, Tim, who Saraya was heading to see now. She hadn't yet figured out what to say to him tonight. Was it fair to him, to either of them, to keep drifting along knowing they were heading nowhere? Saraya supposed not, but it was easy, and there didn't seem to be a lot of exciting alternatives banging down her door either.

He wasn't the one, if there even was such a thing, but it was nice to know he was at the end of the phone if she wanted to talk to someone. Life could feel unbelievably lonely at times, and she wasn't quite ready to lose one more friendly face from her already small circle.

She looked out into the thick darkness of the tunnel rushing by, and wondered how she had found herself here. Her reflection shone back at her, and she stared accusingly into her mirrored eyes.

Her shiny black hair was cut into a chunky pixie cut, tiny silver stars adorning each ear. She wore a fitted black wrap dress, which had dainty blue flowers printed over it in the exact same shade as her shoes and bag. To Saraya, the reflection staring back at her was a disappointment. She couldn't explain what she would have preferred to see, but this wasn't it. She scowled at herself and turned away.

The carriage jerked to a halt, ramming her into the cool, sticky window as the doors hissed open letting a welcome breath of musty, damp air fill the train. Several passengers hurried off, no doubt rushing to get home to their comfortable little lives, Saraya thought enviously.

She spotted a seat halfway down the car and took her chance before someone else could claim it. Sighing with relief, she eased her feet out of her shoes – blue alligator courts – which had been pinching her toes and numbing her soles all day, and arched her stockinged feet gingerly.

The teenager seated beside her listening to his ipod at a deafening volume, leaned away from her with a look of disgust, but the woman in the seat opposite eyed her feet jealously as she tapped her own stilettos in agitation. Saraya offered her an empathetic smile before glancing back along the carriage.

A woman was making her way slowly down the aisle, holding out a cardboard coffee cup as she jangled a few coins in the bottom of it. The woman was quite striking, black hair framed her face, and fell in waves over her shoulders. A long flowing skirt swung low on her hips, grazing filthy, blood streaked, bare feet. Her arms were adorned with cheap gold and silver coloured bangles and her green eyes challenged the passengers to dare to admonish her for begging.

But that was not what caught Saraya's attention so fully. Wrapped in a colourful swathe of fabric, tied close to her chest was a tiny, black haired baby. His bare legs hung free, remarkably clean, though Saraya suspected he must be cold with no socks to warm his tiny feet.

How? she thought. *How did this happen? How could a mother and such a small baby be abandoned by society, forced into trawling through London asking for pitiful handouts?* She could not understand it. Her heart sank as she watched the interactions between the mother and the passengers. She would smile hopefully and hold her cup out towards them, managing to avoid looking aggressive over her desire for a little charity.

The passengers, young and old, business suits

mixed amongst jeans and floral skirts, would inevitably avert their uncomfortable eyes, shrinking back into their seats or staring intently at their feet, refusing to even acknowledge the woman standing before them, until she sighed sadly, her eyes glistening with unspilled tears, and moved away.

Saraya was bowled over by the dignity the mother possessed, her strength to move on and try again and again, despite almost certain rejection. It made her feel guilty to feel so out of control in her own life when she had no good excuse not to do something about it. The woman stopped in front of Saraya and held out her cup.

"Spare some change?" she asked politely.

"Of course," Saraya replied, her hand already digging around in her cavernous blue leather office bag. "How old is he... she?" Saraya asked, gesturing towards the baby.

The woman's face broke into a radiant smile. "He," she confirmed. "He's ten months."

"Really? Oh he's so tiny!" Saraya exclaimed.

"He likes to scrunch himself up and get all cosy

when he's in the sling," the woman replied, rubbing the curve of the baby's spine under the rainbow of material. "He's bigger than he looks. He'll be tall one day, taller than me I wouldn't be surprised," she said, her tone almost defensive, challenging Saraya to disagree.

Saraya smiled, handing her a crumpled twenty pound note. "Do you have somewhere to go? Somewhere to sleep tonight?" she asked softly. The woman across the aisle in the stilettos caught Saraya's eye and shook her head discouragingly. Saraya ignored her.

"That's kind of you to ask. Most people don't." The train slowed as they reached the next stop. "We'll be okay," she said, not answering Saraya's question. The doors opened and she turned, heading towards them.

"Wait," called Saraya as the woman stepped onto the platform. "What's your name?"

"Emily," smiled the mother. "And this is Flynn," she said, cuddling her arms tightly around the baby. "Thank you for this," she smiled holding up the note.

"You're the first person who…" she shook her head and looked down at the baby. "Never mind. But thank you."

Saraya wanted to ask her more. How did she end up on the streets? Where was she going? How could she help? But the doors were sliding closed and Emily was already walking away. The train sped on to the next destination and Saraya realised she had never even told her her own name.

Chapter Four

Finally, thanks to the kindness of the woman on the train, Emily had managed to eat. She'd had bad days in the past two years, but this was turning out to be up there with her worst. Flynn had screamed for an hour solid after the attack in the alley, and though he had escaped without a mark, he was clearly shaken.

After rinsing her own wounds in the tiny sink at yet another public toilet, she had been thankful to realise they would not need stitches. Had she eaten, she would have crawled into her usual spot behind the wheely bins behind Kebab Central and gone to sleep. But her stomach wouldn't let her. Luckily, she had met a rare kindly person who had given her more than she could have hoped for. The remaining money was stowed safely in her backpack, and now in her pocket sat the flick knife, her palm clenched tightly around its handle. She would not make the mistake of letting down her guard again.

She berated herself harshly, thinking of the danger she had put Flynn in. It was obvious that the madman hadn't even registered the presence of an innocent baby there. Perhaps that was for the best, Emily thought fearfully. Who knows how he might have reacted to him. She had a feeling it would not have made him any less violent.

Emily hated that she had put Flynn in danger. Her entire life revolved around keeping him safe. He was the reason she had finally made the decision to walk away from everything she knew and seek solace on the streets of London of all places. She hadn't had any great plan. She just knew that no matter what hardships going it alone may bring, it would have to be better than the life she was living with Karl.

The cocktail of emotions she felt every time she pictured his face was overwhelming, and still after all this time, deeply confusing. She had loved him from the first moment she saw him, with his warm, cheeky face, his twinkling eyes always on the verge of laughter. He had been exactly what she had been looking for.

They had moved in with each other quickly, too quickly her friends had said. But they didn't understand what it was like to finally have someone that was yours. She had been raised in a total of seven different foster homes from the age of five. Her dad had never been a part of her life and she still to this day had no idea of who he was. Her mother had died of an aneurysm on her way to collect Emily from school.

Emily had precious few memories of her mother, but she was sure that the ones she did have were the reason she had survived her childhood. Every now and then, she would remember the feeling of absolute safety she'd had, wrapped under a blanket, her legs entangled with her mother's as they talked in whispers, telling stories, sharing secrets.

She remembered vividly a picnic they'd had. The sun had been warm and the grass was long and tickly on the back of Emily's bare legs as she rested her head in her mother's lap. Whilst she had looked up at the clouds, imagining, her mother had woven daisies into a chain, and braided them through her dark hair. "A crown fit for a princess. *My* princess," she had said, as her fingers stroked their way softly through her tangles. Emily took out that memory as often as she could to prevent it from fading.

So when Karl had offered her love, she had grabbed it with both hands. She had walked blindly into a life together, ignoring the unsettled feeling she got when he sometimes flew off the handle. It always came completely out of the blue, catching her unprepared, but as quickly as it started it was over, and she was left wondering what had happened.

To begin with it was just shouting. Name calling. But as time went by, he got rough. And the strangest thing was that she couldn't pinpoint the first time he hit her. She had already lost so much of herself by that point, already given him so much that it was just the next natural step. He had ground her down until she didn't expect anything else. But despite it all, she would have stayed. She knew she would. Because the ninety percent of the time when she felt as though he loved her, when she felt as if she had a place to call her own, when she could really say she belonged, all made up for the rest.

He cried. Every time. And through his tears he

told her about his childhood. The violence. His dad. The dreaded iron rod. And engulfed in his sobs, she had somehow ended up comforting him. But the more she held him close and tried to help him heal, the more she became his target for releasing his aggression. It had taken her a long time to realise that some people are just too broken to ever put back together.

When she had realised she was carrying his child, things changed in an instant. Here she was, trying to fix this broken boy in the body of a man, but now she had her own child to think of. She wouldn't let him repeat the cycle with her baby. She wouldn't let him hurt her any more.

It had been the most terrifying thing she had ever had to do. She hadn't dared to pack a single bag, for fear of him realising her plan. She'd cut her drivers licence in half, and her bank cards too. She didn't want him to have any way of finding her, even if that meant having to struggle. Her friends had all long since left her life and she had nobody to turn to, but she wasn't going to let that be a reason to stay. She couldn't. Her baby deserved so much more than he would ever be able to offer.

She left her phone on the bedside cabinet and took nothing but the hundred pounds in cash he had given her for the weekly shop. And then, she took a train for the first time in years, travelling from their little town in Kent to London via the most indirect route possible. She hadn't stopped looking over her shoulder the whole way.

Of course, she hadn't bargained on not being able to check into a hostel without any ID. She hadn't realised that leaving her identity behind would make her new life quite so difficult. That first night on the streets was cold, sleepless and eye opening. But harsh as it was, she knew it was right. She couldn't go back. He would kill her.

And now, as she made her way through the growing darkness to her favourite sleeping spot, she realised she didn't have a clue how they were ever going to escape this life. Day to day survival was so consuming, there was no time for anything else. How was she ever going to make enough money to get a roof over their heads? How was she going to give Flynn the life he deserved? She knew she had walked away from a life of terror, but into what?

She began to make her way over the busy crossroad, and suddenly stopped dead in her tracks. *Karl.* It was him. There by the traffic lights over the opposite side of the road. It *had to* be him, she would know him anywhere. Forcing herself to stay calm, she stepped backwards, trying to melt away from view. *Was it him?* She wanted to move closer, to get a better view of his face to make sure, but she couldn't risk hanging around to find out. He hadn't yet spotted her and she didn't want to wait until he did.

Turning, she tripped on the stairs leading down into the underground bypass, catching hold of the smooth steel rail to steady herself. She took the stairs two at a time, looking behind her as she ran, her arms knotted tightly around her precious baby. She sprinted flat out, terror flooding through her. She had to protect Flynn, she had to get away from here. She rounded a corner and gasped as she collided with something solid. Looking up, she let out a scream of terror as she realised who she was staring at. It was the mad man from the alley.

"Hello, Dollybird," he laughed wickedly, leaning into her face, his stale breath making her reel back. The sound of her scream lasted only a second, before she saw the glint of the blade. As it ripped across her jugular, one thought carried her into oblivion. *I'm sorry, Flynn. I failed.*

Chapter Five

It had rained in the thirty minutes Saraya had been on the underground, and the pavements were shiny and wet. Muddy droplets splashed upwards as she strolled towards her destination, leaving swirling patterns on her shoes and ankles. She shivered, her body adjusting to the cool air after the heat of the tube.

It was only a short walk to Tim's flat and as she always did, she wondered if she had the energy for her visit. Her heels clacked on the pavement as she walked, deep in thought, the image of the mother and baby still etched on her mind. She wondered where they were now, if she was using the money to get some hot food. If the baby was cold.

She stepped out to cross the road and narrowly missed colliding with a cyclist who swore loudly in her direction as he raced by. She huffed audibly, and then quickened her step as the rain began to fall in heavy drops once again, pressing the buzzer and waiting for the familiar sound of Tim's voice inviting her up.

Even coming here was routine, Saraya thought, as she hung her damp coat on the hook beside the door and sighed. Tim's flat was warm and cosy, and much as she hated to admit it, she always felt comfortable there. Just like always, he poured a glass of wine for her as she dialled the number for their regular sushi restaurant and ordered the usual. "So," he smiled, handing her the wine and kissing her briefly on the mouth. "How was your day?"

"Same as ever," she shrugged unenthusiastically. "Long, arduous..." Tim snorted. "What was that?" Saraya asked

"What?"

"You laughed."

"I just think you're funny, that's all," Tim smiled, rolling his eyes and taking a sip of his own wine.

"Funny how?" Saraya probed, feeling irritable.

"Oh, it doesn't matter," Tim shrugged, kissing her on the forehead and heading back to the kitchen. Saraya stood up and followed him, taking her glass with her. Tim was opening cupboards and drawers, pulling out plates and chopsticks.

"No, go on. Funny how?" she pushed.

"You really want to know?"

"Yes."

Tim turned, looking her right in the eye. She flinched at the intimacy, glancing away. He sighed and continued. "Okay, well if you must know, I just think it's funny how you always complain about your day, you never seem to feel fulfilled or satisfied by your work, and yet you never do anything to change it. You do the same thing, you get the same result," he said simply.

"Oh, as if it's that simple," Saraya bit back. "I'm sure I'd be much happier sitting on a sunshiny beach in the tropics, sipping margaritas all day, but there's this thing called money which seems to be an issue." She put a hand on her hip defensively. "You can't tell me you're happy all the time?"

"Nobody's happy all of the time," Tim replied gently. "But I would say that I'm happy most of the time. I hated that job at the bank, so I left it and now I enjoy what I do. No I'm never going to be rich as a social worker, but I love it and I feel good at the end of a long day. I know I'm making a difference and that means more to me than any amount of money. He placed a gentle hand on her shoulder. "You say you can't do what you want because of money, but that's an excuse. I know you've got close to twenty grand in your savings account."

"Twenty grand is nothing these days," Saraya replied. "And besides, I'm saving that for my future."

"What for? What is it that you'll do then that you can't do now?" he asked. "What, you want to save your pennies so you can keep dreaming about a future that might never happen? What's the bloody point?" he asked almost angrily. "If you're not happy now, what makes you think you will be then?"

"I don't know," Saraya admitted. "But that's the way it goes, isn't it? We suffer when we're young so we can reap the benefits when we're old."

"And waste your whole life waiting for a few good years at the end," Tim scoffed. "When you'll probably be too jaded and too tired to do anything anyway."

Saraya started to speak but the doorbell rang and Tim went to pay for their food. He came back and served them each some sushi, which they ate at the breakfast bar in silence. Saraya picked at hers thoughtfully. Much as she hated to admit it, Tim had a point. It wasn't right that she should be so miserable, but she didn't know what to do about it, how to even begin to start changing things for the positive. She looked up at him. "You're right," she said quietly. "I know you're right, but what do I do?"

"What do you *want* to do?"

"I don't know. I don't know how to break out of this trap I've set for myself."

"Start small. What do you really want from life?" Tim asked, setting down his chopsticks and taking her hand.

She sighed. "I just don't know. That's the problem. I don't know what I want."

"Then that's your first step. Figure out what you want," his face broke into a smile. "Then you can figure out how to get it."

"You make it sound so easy."

"It is if you let it be. Just open your eyes. Stop plodding along on a path you don't even want to be on and do something that means something to you. Something real."

Saraya looked at him and wondered if that something would include him. She couldn't picture a future with him, but she decided not to say anything for tonight. He had given her a lot to think about and she didn't want to ruin their evening.

"We'll see," she smiled.

"Yes, we will," he grinned back. "But first, eat your sushi," he said, pouring more soy sauce for her. "That's good fish you're wasting there!"

Chapter Six

Saraya had left Tim's flat engrossed in her thoughts, telling him she would call in a few days. He hadn't pushed for her to stay over and she was grateful he hadn't asked. It was dark by the time she neared the underground station and she hesitated, looking apprehensively at the gloomy steps leading down to a deserted, enclosed alley – the bypass which avoided having to navigate the continued thick traffic of the crossroad.

Glancing behind her to check she wasn't being followed, she made her decision and walked briskly down the stairs. There was, as always, a strong smell of urine in the air, along with a smattering of broken glass and empty food packets. There was no sound but the whistling of the wind through the tunnel and the echo of her heels on the cracked paving slabs. Or was there?

Saraya stopped still, her breathing shallow as she cocked an ear, waiting. A moment passed. And then she heard it. The unmistakable cry of a baby. Where was it coming from? The cry came again, now more frantic, and this time it didn't stop.

Without thinking, Saraya followed it, the sound pulling her deeper into the tunnel. Up ahead to the left she could see an alcove cut into the stone, and as she approached she was sure the baby was inside it. She hurried now, her palms sweating, fear for what she might find radiating through her.

Pausing just outside the gloomy recess, she peered in cautiously. It was dark inside, but the dim lights from the roof of the tunnel shone just enough to illuminate the small nook. The space was around five feet wide and ten feet deep, a little man-made cave of sorts. The floor was covered in old newspapers, one thin threadbare blanket screwed up in a ball against the wall. A puddle of dark, sticky liquid pooled by the entrance and trailed towards the back of the alcove, where a body lay slumped on its side on the hard stone floor, its back facing her.

"Oh my god," Saraya breathed. "Hello?" she called, trying to rouse the figure. "Hello? Can you hear me?" The body remained unmoving, but the cries intensified. Looking back along the tunnel to check she was alone, Saraya took a deep breath and stepped inside, carefully avoiding the pool of blood. She took her phone from her pocket and switched on the torch, illuminating the space and casting eerie shadows on the walls. She angled it towards the back and gasped.

It was her, the woman from the train. The mother! Saraya rushed forward, placing a hand on her shoulder and rolling her onto her back. "Emily! Emily, can you hear me?" Saraya yelled frantically.

"Oh my god!" she repeated in horror. "Oh, Emily, no!" The baby, Flynn, was still wrapped to her chest, his arms waving desperately as he pushed his blood splattered hands against his mother. Emily was, even to Saraya's untrained eye, quite obviously dead. Her eyes were wide and dry, and a deep long slash ran diagonally from her left ear, down across her throat. The blood surrounding the wound was dry and crusted.

Saraya swayed, and then fell, her knees hitting stone, her hands grazing harshly against it. Her mouth filled with bile and she held back the vomit which was threatening to come. Still the baby screamed. *He's tied to a corpse!* Saraya suddenly thought in disgust. "Oh Flynn, poor little Flynn!"

She crawled towards him, her hands scrambling to untie the complicated arrangement of material, until finally she found the knot and worked to release it. The metallic smell of stale blood filled her nostrils, and she gagged as she pulled the squirming baby out of the layers of plasma soaked cloth and into her trembling arms.

He was cold and wet, but as she held him close, at last his pitiful sobs abated. He looked into her eyes for a long moment, before he gave a shaky sigh of exhaustion and faded into unconsciousness. Saraya felt his tiny body soften, content in the knowledge that he was safe at last. She stared at his pale, sleeping face for a moment, shock paralysing her.

A tremor rocked through Flynn's body and shook her from her stupor. She stood, her arms still firm around him, and stumbled towards the discarded blanket, shaking it out and swaddling him snugly in it.

It smelled like rotting vegetables and wet dogs, but at least it was warm and mostly dry. Saraya turned to stare at Emily. She wanted to do something, to make her more comfortable somehow, but she knew that it was a ridiculous thought. There was no helping her now.

A sob escaped from her throat and bounced off the walls echoing loudly. And then, another sound – footsteps, reached her ears, accompanied by laughter, shouting. People were coming. She pulled the bundle protectively against her chest and crouched down beside Emily. "I'll take care of him," she whispered. "I promise."

And with that vow lingering in the air, she turned and ran, away from the sound of approaching voices and away from the woman who had unintentionally changed her life in the course of a day.

Chapter Seven

What have I done? Saraya thought in panic as she turned the key to her flat and slipped inside, slamming the door behind her. She entered the sitting room and approached the ornate teal table lamp, flicking the switch and sinking heavily into her favourite armchair beside the window. She looked out at the deserted road, the street-lights casting a soft orange glow over the glistening tarmac. She half expected to see police cars racing up the road after her, blue lights slicing through the peaceful neighbourhood.

The bundle in her arms whimpered and rolled closer to her warmth, his eyes opening briefly to stare at her with groggy confusion, before the urge to sleep grew too powerful and he snuggled into her chest, his eyes sinking slowly closed once again. Saraya's heart was pounding, her palms were dripping with sweat, and her body shook violently. She was sure she was going into a state of shock, but didn't know what she should do.

As her teeth began to chatter, she suddenly remembered Steve. He had been a fling from three, or was it four years previously? A St. John's ambulance driver with broad shoulders and a tendency towards casual racism. It hadn't lasted long. But as Saraya shuddered in the dim glow of her Laura Ashley lamp, she remembered a story he had told her about a car accident he'd been called to before one of their few dates.

The driver had been a woman who had gone over some black ice, skidding into the central reservation at eighty five miles per hour. The car had been flipped on its roof and her husband, who had forgotten his seatbelt was thrown right through the windscreen. He was decapitated. A very clean break Steve had said, painting a picture Saraya could have done without, over her spinach soufflé.

The woman had, by some miracle, managed to avoid any physical injury, but on seeing her husband she had unsurprisingly gone into acute shock. Steve had relayed to Saraya how important it had been to get her warm and to keep her legs elevated to keep the blood going to the vital organs. She remembered how angry he had become when she'd suggested a cup of hot sweet tea might have been in order. "Are you mad! Not unless you want to kill her outright," he'd growled across the table.

Saraya shivered again. She spun in the armchair, careful not to disturb the sleeping baby, and hung her legs over the arm. She pulled a throw from the back of the chair and flung it over herself and the baby, snuggling down into it. She listened to Flynn's slow, rhythmic breathing and tried to match her own to his pattern. Very slowly she began to feel a sense of calm settle over her. The trembling faded away and her thoughts became clearer in her jumbled mind.

Ever so gently she slipped off the chair and onto her knees, bending low to place Flynn on the sheepskin rug. He remained sleeping. With careful fingers she eased back his musty blanket to look at him. Her breath caught in her throat as she assessed his condition. The grubby grey of his vest was barely visible under the rusty brown splashes of dried blood. His face was crusted and filthy and even his tiny eyelashes had stuck together in clumps.

The moisture evaporated from her mouth and her hands trembled as she stared in horror at him, trying to understand the world he had come from. What kind of person would hurt a mother, much less one holding her baby? What had Emily been involved in? Was it a fluke unfortunate encounter or was she killed by someone she knew?

Saraya closed her eyes, picturing Emily lying there on the cold hard concrete, trying to imagine how terrified she must have been in the moments before her death. She wondered if that grotty hole was where they usually slept, vulnerable to any lunatic who happened to walk by. Indecision flooded her now. Should she go to the police, report what she knew? She knew she should, of course that was the right thing to do, but somewhere deep inside her, conflict raged.

A strange new feeling was bubbling up inside her and Saraya felt herself taken aback by the strength of it.

I want him.

She clapped her hand over her mouth, her eyes wide as she struggled with the enormity of what she was considering. She couldn't keep a baby she had found on the streets, no matter what the circumstances. In her final words to the cold, blood soaked body of Emily, she had promised that she would take care of her baby, and she had meant it. But what did that even mean? Taking him to the police and getting him into a foster home? She shuddered, her fists clenching with surprising resistance at the thought of placing him in a strangers arms and walking away. She couldn't do it. *I want him.*

But the world doesn't work like that, she thought despairingly. It has to be done properly. Paperwork filled in, courses attended, money handed over too, no doubt. And why would they even consider her as a guardian for Flynn? She had no ties to him, no experience caring for children. They would say no. She was certain of it.

But what if... she wondered, her thoughts trickling like molasses through her mind as she worked through the predicament. "What if I didn't tell them?" she whispered to the empty room. Her head began to spin with the possibility of it. Nobody knows he is here. Nobody is going to be looking for him. He was alone on the streets and his mother is dead. Who's going to stand in my way? Fire ignited in her belly as she felt her lips twitch at the corners, a slow smile breaking across her blood streaked face.

"I want him," she said with conviction. She had never felt so sure of anything in her whole life. She had sworn to Emily that she would take care of him and she intended to keep that promise. Looking at his fragile little body Saraya realised that for the first time in her life, she knew exactly what she wanted, something she had never expected or admitted to herself. She wanted to be a mother. Flynn's mother.

Chapter Eight

There was literally nothing in the whole flat to dress a baby in. Saraya pulled open drawers, rummaging through them with no success, tossing jeans and cashmere jumpers aside. She pulled out an old brushed cotton nightie and frowned as she looked at it. "It will have to do," she muttered. She threw it onto the bed on top of the pile of towels she'd placed there and sighed. Tomorrow, she would have to go shopping, but changing Flynn couldn't wait until then.

Saraya headed to the kitchen and turned on the tap. Her own hands were crusted in dried blood, and her stomach lurched as she soaped and rinsed them again and again. When they were finally clean, she continued to let the tap run, filling a washing up bowl with warm water as she stripped off her dress and threw it in the washing machine, turning it on to ninety degrees and adding far more detergent than was necessary.

The water rose and thick white foamy bubbles tumbled, engulfing the dress. Saraya watched it, realising she would never wear it again no matter how clean it looked. Emily's blood would always be ingrained in the depths of the fabric. She should have burned it.

She tiptoed back into the living room to check on Flynn, who was still sleeping soundly on the rug. She had covered him with the throw and turned the heating on high. She backed out of the room quietly and headed for the shower, stopping to turn the kitchen tap off on her way.

The water burned hot as she scrubbed at her body, her hair, the feeling of someone else's fluids permeating her skin deeper than soap could cleanse. The shock of the evening had begun to wear off, and now Saraya felt utterly drained. The picture of Emily on the train, beautiful and vibrant walking bravely towards her and asking unashamedly for Saraya's charity burned brightly in her mind. What a cruel waste of life. It was still hard to fathom how quickly it had ended. How she could have been there one minute, then gone so brutally, in the blink of an eye. Saraya couldn't stop thinking about what kind of person it would take to kill a mother still holding her innocent baby. Whoever it was, whatever it was over, there could be no justification for their actions. Her eyes filled with tears as she thought of the fear she had seen in Flynn's dark eyes when she had lifted him from his mother's lifeless body.

As if the flowing water could mask them, she let her heavy tears flow, her emotions wildly confused and inconsistent. She sobbed for Flynn who would never know or remember his mother. For the scars on his heart he would bear his whole life, which she would never be able to erase and that he would never fully understand.

She sobbed for poor Emily, knowing how desperate her last gasps must have been, how unbearable it must have felt to know she was fading away and that she could no longer protect her child. Her thoughts moved to the cold dark streets beyond her window, and she wondered with sadness how many other mothers were out there right now, fighting for their children, going hungry so their babies wouldn't.

And then, her tears transformed from the heavy weight of despair, to those of indescribable joy. She *would* keep him. Nothing had ever felt so right. She choked on tears of elation, knowing that her life was finally worthwhile, that she had something of meaning to do, someone who she would matter to. She sobbed until the tears ran dry and her body ached with exhaustion, finally turning off the shower and stepping red raw and jelly legged out into the steam of the bathroom.

Next, after dressing herself in the thickest pyjamas she could find, she headed back to collect the bowl of water from the kitchen, a fluffy purple towel and the cotton nightie tucked under her arm. She added some more hot water to the bowl, swirling it with her fingertips, then threw an old flannel into it. With gentle footsteps she made her way back to the still slumbering Flynn, setting her load on the wooden floorboards beside the rug.

She paused, watching his fragile little face, his pouted lips sucking the air as he dreamed of milk no doubt. She hated to disturb him, but it had to be done. The horror of the evening was displayed across his skin and Saraya couldn't stand to leave him in this state one moment longer.

Gently she unpopped his now stiff vest and eased it slowly upwards over his stomach. His breath caught and a whimper escaped his lips as he raised a grubby fist to rub deeply at his eyes.

"It's okay, baby, it's okay," Saraya soothed in a sing song voice. At the sound of the unfamiliar tone, Flynn's eyes shot open. He stared wide eyed at Saraya, silent and wary. "It's okay, Flynn. I'll look after you," she whispered gently. She took the flannel from the bowl and wrung it out. Peeling his arms and head out of the vest and flinging his sodden nappy on top of it, she lowered the cloth down to wash his face. "I'm just going to clean you up a bit sweetie. You're very – " The second the flannel touched him, Flynn let out a blood-curdling scream. His legs kicked out at her, his arms flailed wildly and he tried desperately to roll away from her touch.

Saraya felt panic course through her veins as his piercing cries grew louder still. She tried to calm him, singing a lullaby while attempting to work quickly to remove the blood. She dabbed at his face, not wanting to aggravate his delicate skin, but making no progress. His hair was matted, the blood dry and thick covering every inch of him. The damp wash-cloth was useless.

Flynn bellowed, then sucked in a breath and went silent. Staring at him she watched in terror as his lips turned blue. "Flynn!" she cried. "Flynn, breathe!" She held him up and gasped as he continued to hold the breath. "Flynn!" she screamed, patting her palm furiously against his back. She felt his muscles beginning to grow limp and made a sudden decision. She turned him towards her, bringing his mouth inches from hers, took a deep breath and blew straight into his pale scrunched up face. He blinked, gasped and finally released an almighty wail.

"Oh, thank god!" Saraya exclaimed, leaning heavily against the sofa. She sighed with relief, watching the colour return to his lips. "I prefer the screaming to that." He hiccuped and then began to cry again. Clearly, this wasn't going to be easy.

Shakily, she pulled the bowl of water closer and pursed her lips. "I'm really sorry about this, little one, but I think quicker is going to be better for both of us." She held him as gently as she could without dropping the thrashing, furious bundle, and in one quick move she lowered him into the bowl, the water settling around his shoulders. He screamed and kicked, but she knew she couldn't stop now. It would only mean trying again in a few minutes. Much better to get it over and done with, she thought grimly.

The blood came away easily now and she wiped the cloth over him, humming softly, hoping the melody was helping in some small way. The soft tune seemed to help her focus on the task at hand at the very least. After just a few minutes he was pink and clean. Without lingering, she pulled him, still wailing, from the makeshift bath and wrapped him snugly in the towel, cradling him against her chest to soothe him.

She stood, holding him close and warm, swaying gently as his cries finally began to ease. "I'm sorry, baby, I'm sorry. But the worst is over," she told him, hoping her words were true. Flynn yawned and leaned his downy head against her chest. Saraya suddenly felt overwhelmingly tired too. Leaving the dirty water and clothes on the living room floor, she picked up the nightdress and carried the baby through to her bedroom, placing him down on top of the duvet.

Quickly she pulled the nightie over his head and knotted it below his feet, fashioning a DIY sleeping bag. "That will do," she muttered. She pulled back the bed covers and folded the towel, placing it on the mattress and transferring the sleepy baby onto it. "I have a feeling we're both going to get covered in wee tonight," she sighed. "Shopping tomorrow, sweetie."

She climbed into bed beside him and he rolled towards her, his forehead resting on her arm. The smell of his scalp was clean and pure. She placed her hand softly on his abdomen and watched his eyes drifting closed. "We're going to be okay, angel. We are," she whispered into the darkness, unsure if it was Flynn or herself she was trying to reassure.

A tear slid slowly down her cheek and landed, glistening, on the forehead of the sleeping baby.

Saraya pulled him closer and felt herself being dragged into the sweet escape of sleep as she was carried far away from the nightmare of the evening.

Chapter Nine

If there was a topic Saraya could call herself an expert on, it would be domestic adoption in Britain. She knew innumerable facts, anecdotes, personal accounts and statistics. She could tell you that at any given time in the United Kingdom, there are almost seventy thousand children under the care of local authorities. Seventy thousand children without a family to call their own, without the security of a mother and father who are theirs unconditionally.

She could also tell you that out of those seventy thousand children, just five thousand will go on to find their forever family. The remaining sixty-five thousand children just wait. And perhaps some of them manage to hold onto hope as each year passes and their chances of being pulled from the ugly system grow slimmer.

These statistics, which ran through her mind on a regular basis, were comforting somehow. The numbers made her feel like she had some semblance of control and understanding over her life. She had never shared them, not even with Tim. She'd never made use of them. But she knew them by heart. She made it her business to know them. She devoured them, tried to make sense of them, and grasp hold of them. Because for the first seven years of her life, she had been one of those seventy thousand children. A number on the system, a child without a proper family. She knew exactly what it meant to wait. She knew exactly how those lost children felt.

They wait. And they hope. But most will never find their way home.

Saraya woke with a start and sat bolt upright, her eyes wide and bleary. A fine film of sweat coated her forehead, and she wiped it away with the back of her hand. The colours and shapes of her dream were already beginning to fade but she could still feel the after effects of it. Too much blood, dark silhouettes chasing her through an ever shrinking tunnel, their wicked blades glinting as they gained on her and the precious bundle she carried.

Flynn.

She turned to see him grunting and wriggling in his sleep. It wouldn't be long before he woke. A dim light was just beginning to filter through the half closed curtains and Saraya picked up the bedside clock. Six a.m. She sighed and stretched, climbing out of bed and pulling on a soft pair of jeans and a crumpled t-shirt. Quickly she tiptoed to the bathroom, dragging a brush through her hair and loading her toothbrush with paste. A cry echoed through the hallway and she dropped it unused into the sink, rushing into the bedroom. Flynn stared accusingly up at her.

"Morning, baby," she smiled. "Don't worry, I didn't go anywhere, I'm not leaving you, darling." Flynn squeaked and chewed his fist angrily. "You're hungry," Saraya noted with a frown. She pulled back the duvet to find the towel and nightie sodden with urine. "Just as I'd expected," she muttered. She peeled back the layers until he was free of the damp material and smiled with relief. "No number two at least."

She carried him into the bathroom and ran a sink full of warm water, giving him a quick wipe down.

Swaddling him in a clean towel, she looked him in the eye. "This clothing situation is looking a bit desperate, isn't it?" He grunted and began to grizzle, arching stiffly away from her as she tried to hold him safely. His limbs were rigid with tension, and Saraya tried to keep her hold loose, not forcing him to lean into her body against his will. She could see fear and uncertainty in his expression as he watched her suspiciously. "Okay," she said softly. "Let's find you something to eat."

Holding him gently, she walked purposefully to the kitchen and opened the fridge, appraising the contents inside. It was embarrassingly bare and she silently berated herself for not being more domestic. Although, it was no doubt better than the spread he was used to on the streets. She blinked away the image of Emily that came to mind and forced herself to focus on the task at hand. "Well, looks like I'm Old Mother Hubbard, hey Flynn?" A half eaten Crunchie, a punnet of cherries and a chocolate pudding were strewn across the shelves. Moving the chocolate pudding aside, she found a tub of natural yoghurt, still sealed and in date. "Excellent!" she smiled. "This will do, won't it?"

Flynn kicked and began to cry, his little fists pummelling against her chest as she searched in a drawer for a teaspoon. His face grew redder and redder as she struggled to hold him and peel back the lid of the yoghurt. "Hold on, baby, hold on, it's coming," she placated. She dipped the spoon into the thick white gloop and held it to his mouth. Flynn waved his hands up and down frantically, his mouth open wide in desperation.

The yoghurt touched his tongue and silenced him immediately. He swallowed and searched around for more. She dipped the spoon again. Saraya breathed a sigh of relief as he devoured his fill. His frenzied eating gradually slowed and as the bottom of the pot became visible, he finally leaned back, satisfied for the moment. Saraya lifted the spoon to his mouth one final time, scraping the edge of it across his tiny lips, clearing the last traces of yoghurt from them.

She placed the empty tub on the table and turned him on her lap so he was facing her. He wriggled and kicked his legs. The towel he was cocooned in fell loose settling around his waist, his full belly protruding over the top of the folds. Flynn was silent as he focused on her, his expression serious and questioning, his tiny head bobbing to the side as he took everything in. Saraya wasn't sure if she should do something. Her experience with babies was limited to the time she had spent with her older sister's two children, and that amounted to very little.

She had actually been giddy with excitement when she had heard the news that Coralie was pregnant and she was going to have her first niece. She had pictured her sister becoming less of the brusque, moody character, with no time for anything except her career, and more soft around the edges, easier to be around. She had hoped that the two of them would grow closer, take the baby to the park together and laugh as they rediscovered the games of their own childhood, passing them on to the next generation.

Yet it hadn't worked out that way. Coralie had tackled motherhood with the same level of control as she had always enjoyed over her life. When Saraya had tried to cuddle Beatrix, Coralie had firmly reprimanded her for interfering with her nap routine and spoiling the child with her coddling. When she had offered to babysit when Coralie and her husband Graham had wanted to go to the theatre, she had been scoffed at and told they had a nanny for that sort of thing and she wouldn't know what to do with a baby anyway. *It's not something you can just do, Saraya! Motherhood is a skill.*

Saraya had felt her excitement slowly ebbing away, replaced with a deep sadness as it dawned on her that her sister didn't really want Saraya to be a part of her children's lives. She would not be getting the close bond she had hoped for, with either her sister or her niece. She learned to stop asking for time with her. She learned to stop buying gifts, because every time she did she was told it was the wrong thing.

By the time Coralie had her second baby, Jamie, Saraya was already too prepared for rejection to allow herself to feel anything but ambivalence about him. They were beautiful, adorable children, but she didn't know them at all. It was easier to pretend not to care.

But here in her arms was a baby she *did* have a chance with. A baby who would no doubt turn her life upside down, but she couldn't think of anything better. She would pick him up at every opportunity. She would cuddle him as much as he needed. She would get to play, to show him the games she didn't get to share with her niece and nephew, to take him places where he could get muddy and covered in grass stains and have the fun he deserved.

She pictured the horror on Coralie's face the time Saraya had placed a crawling Beatrix down on the grass in white dungarees. The poor child had barely had chance to run her fingers through the silky blades, before she had been scooped up and moved to her baby seat where she, *"wouldn't get filthy."*

"I promise, I will never stop you learning about the world because I'm worried about a silly pair of dungarees," she told Flynn seriously now. "You never need to worry about that." She tentatively leaned forward and kissed his forehead. He was still watching her with intense focus.

Saraya assumed that he was feeling very confused.

Wondering when his mother would come for him, no doubt. It hurt to think of how strong his yearning for her must be. A tightness gripped her chest as she looked into his eyes, wishing more than anything that she could take his pain and make this easier for him.

A few seconds passed. He looked on the verge of tears and Saraya found herself instinctively puffing out her cheeks, blowing a loud raspberry at him. She smiled hopefully and then suddenly, he broke into the most radiant smile Saraya had ever seen. He was utterly transformed, his cheeks dimpled and round with joy as he brought a clammy hand up to her face, touching her nose, her lips, exploring her as he accepted her presence in his life. Saraya couldn't breathe. She held still, a statue as he continued to poke and pat at her, unwilling to let the moment end.

She grinned, affection coursing through her whole being, flowing in waves through her blood as she watched his intense concentration. He seized the opportunity to delve into her mouth, grabbing at her teeth, then anchoring his fingers over the bottom row pulling her mouth wide open. Saraya let out a burst of laughter at the thought of how ridiculous she must look, and gently removed his chubby hand, wiping it against her t-shirt.

"Hello, Flynn," she said quietly, her heart soaring at the relaxed expression on his little face. He looked like an angel, a cherub and she felt a rush of love like she had never felt before. She stroked a silky finger down his cheek and chuckled as he grabbed for it, bringing it to his mouth.

So this was parenting. Huh. For some reason, having her own children had never been at the forefront of her thoughts. Though her experience with her sister's children had been mostly down to Coralie's need for absolute control, she had come away from it wary of what being a parent really involved. Did it have to be so stressful? Coralie never really seemed happy in her role as a mother, and frequently complained about everything she couldn't do now.

Saraya had grown to fear the ties that came with having children. She liked the knowledge that she was free. If she wanted to, she could get up at noon and eat junk food all day. Go to all night raves in abandoned warehouses, jump up at a moments notice and jet off to the other side of the world. She could accept any invitation that came her way and never have to consider any small person who was relying on her. She could dance under the moonlight and sit around bonfires drinking warm rum and talking into the wee hours. You certainly couldn't do that with children.

Yet this notion of freedom she held so dear to, was nothing but that. A notion. She didn't travel. She didn't go to wild parties until four a.m. She didn't live spontaneously, seize the day or do anything out of the ordinary. She was utterly boring. Tim was right. She hadn't made the most of her time on this earth. If she had suddenly dropped dead, there would be no one to remember her, no legacy to leave. She had nothing to be proud of, nothing to put her name to, and she would be quickly forgotten.

Maybe being forgotten wasn't so bad, she pondered as Flynn kicked his legs trying to snuggle closer to her. After all, everyone is forgotten eventually. It's not the being remembered that matters, more the knowledge that during her time on this planet, *she* had mattered. That she had made a positive impact to the world in some tiny way. That she had really and truly lived, not just existed.

As Flynn settled down to sleep in her arms, sucking wetly at the side of his fist, she realised that she had never been brave. Not once had she taken a risk and done something terrifying. She'd said no again and again. Thought up excuses and brushed off opportunities, even though any one of those paths could have led her on the adventure she'd been searching for. The thing that would change her life. She had cowered away, taken the easy route, hidden from challenge and as a result, she had spent the last decade – if not more – feeling like a lost soul, unsure why her life had no depth or meaning, yet too afraid to do anything to change her circumstances.

Well not any longer. Maybe she had finally gone crazy. Maybe. But for the very first time, she had finally taken a risk and stepped onto the path of uncertainty. And it felt more right than anything she had ever done before. It was true that children had never been a part of her plan, but why should that matter? Plans change, and even the best ones sometimes fall off course. As she smiled down at the dark haired baby in her arms, she found herself pondering questions she'd never dared to consider before. Why do we always have to be in control? To plan and lay out exactly what we expect from life, until there are no surprises left? Why can't we give in and say yes, follow our gut and do the thing that feels right, even if it's not the simple choice? If we don't take chances, we may as well curl up and die right this moment.

Saraya knew, deep within her belly that this was right. She could end up in prison. She could lose him. She knew with absolute certainty that she would die before she let anyone hurt him. She was his and she would go to the end of the world to protect him. She was taking a risk, and it could end in absolute disaster, but for the first time in her life, she simply didn't care. Her life was worthless without him and she wouldn't give him up.

Smiling down at him as he tilted his head back and gave a little snore, she knew she would continue along this path without turning back. Flynn was her legacy and through being his mother, she would make a difference in the world.

Chapter Ten

Tesco at six-thirty a.m was a new experience. A few people pottered about, an elderly gentleman perusing the newspapers, and a man in a suit picking up a pre-packed BLT and a carton of orange juice, but mostly it was just the washed out faces of the night staff keen to go home to their beds who Saraya encountered. With a sleeping Flynn double wrapped in thick blankets and bundled into the baby seat in the trolley, Saraya made her way inexpertly through the aisles, avoiding eye contact with everyone she passed.

Making for the baby aisle, she threw teddies and rattles, muslins and dummies into the trolley, before turning to find a sea of formula and nappies. "Why do there have to be so many bloody types?" she muttered grumpily. Reading the cans of baby milk, she shook her head in confusion, settling on one that claimed to be, "The best alternative to breast milk."

"I doubt you've ever had anything like this before, have you, sweetie?" she said to the sleeping baby with a frown. She chose some bottles and then settled on nappies which claimed to be chemical free. Then she threw dozens of pouches of baby food in alongside her loot.

Next she headed to the clothes department, running her fingers over soft little baby-grows and adorable dungarees. She picked one of everything, holding them up against him to check the size. Although Emily had said he was ten months old, he looked to be closer to six months in clothing.

Saraya suddenly realised that she didn't know the date of Flynn's birthday. How awful for him never to know the date he was born. She counted on her fingers, surmising he must have been born in January or perhaps December. Based on his size she wouldn't have been surprised if he had been an early baby. I'll just have to pick a date myself, she decided firmly. He deserves a proper birthday and he'll get one.

She was just pushing the trolley out of the clothing department when she spotted a shelf filled with squishy faced soft cotton dolls. She found herself drawn to it, as if by magnetic force. There, in the centre of the shelf was a sweet black haired doll who looked exactly like her squishy cheeked Flynn. It reminded her of the old cabbage patch dolls her and her sister used to carry about everywhere, only this one was much cuter.

She picked it up in wonder, holding it beside him as she marvelled at the similarity. "What a sweet doll!" she exclaimed. "A twin for you, Flynn." She tucked it into the seat beside him and chuckled as Flynn turned his face towards it, his lips resting on the dolls soft cheek.

Saraya paced back and forth outside the department store, waiting for it to open. In her haste she had washed and dressed Flynn, fed him a bottle of milk and a bowl of spinach and potato purée and tucked him under her coat, heading back into the world once again, her handbag stuffed with nappies, wipes, spare babygrows and two full bottles for the journey. She needed to buy the big stuff now. A pushchair, a car seat, maybe one of those Moses basket things. She hadn't realised that it wasn't yet eight a.m and the shops weren't open.

Flynn was surprisingly heavy in her arms and she felt her fingers begin to prickle as he leaned against her forearm cutting off her circulation. She shifted his weight and wandered further along the road in agitation. A woman was opening a door, turning the sign from "Closed" to "Welcome" and Saraya broke into a smile as she realised what she was looking at. A baby boutique!

The woman turned to look at her as she approached, and Saraya smiled nervously, shielding Flynn's face from view. "Excuse me, do you sell pushchairs?" Saraya enquired. "I need a new one, mine... broke yesterday, and this little one is too heavy to carry."

"We do indeed, come in," the woman replied with a smile. She flicked her shoulder length grey hair out of her eyes and Saraya followed her swishing skirts as she headed back inside. The shop was a world of baby furniture. *More than any baby could ever need,* Saraya thought. Beautiful oak child sized wardrobes, drawers and cots were on display along one wall. There were row upon row of shining silver prams, soft creamy blankets and beautifully woven Moses baskets. Saraya was overwhelmed. She looked at it all in amazement.

"So what kind of thing are you looking for?" the woman asked.

"Um, I'm not really sure. I don't think he would like these ones," she said, gesturing to the massive Silver Cross prams. "I think he'd like to sit up and see the world. But be able to lie down for a sleep too. Do you have anything like that?"

"Of course. Let me see. Now do you want it to be parent facing?"

"Parent facing?"

"Yes, you know, with the baby facing you rather than outwards. A lot of parents prefer it."

"Yes, that sounds okay, I think I'd like that."

She nodded. "Now just give me a moment and I'll pop out the back. I think I have just the thing." Saraya nodded and watched her leave. She wandered over to look at the baskets and cots, wondering if Flynn would like to sleep in one of them. There was something quite primal about having him sleep in her arms, and she wasn't sure he needed a bed of his own. Maybe just for naps, she pondered as she saw a pretty white basket on a wooden rocking stand.

The bell rang making her jump, and she turned to see two women entering the shop, both around sixty and deep in conversation with one another. Saraya offered up a shy smile and turned back to the basket. Flynn was beginning to get fussy. He started kicking his legs hard, trying to escape the confines of her coat. Quickly, trying to placate him, she unzipped it and popped him on her hip, letting him look around.

The ladies stopped talking the moment they saw him. Approaching with speed they both began cooing and grinning at him. Flynn gurgled and smiled and Saraya silently cursed him for encouraging them over. She hadn't yet had chance to see the news, for all she knew Flynn and Emily were on the front page. Her stomach clenched as they stopped to fawn over him.

"Well isn't he a sweetie," the taller of the two was saying. "What's his name?"

"Um, Flynn," she replied, caught off guard.

"Flynn. Gorgeous! I love his hair, it's so fluffy and so dark. He takes after you."

"Really?" Saraya looked at him in surprise.

"Yes dear, he does. Look at those eyes. His mother's eyes."

Saraya felt pride bloom inside her as she looked at the baby in her arms. There was a tinge of hazel around the iris that she hadn't noticed before, a feature they both shared. And they both had rich chocolaty hair. She could see why they would find a resemblance. Saraya beamed in pleasure taking joy in their compliments. She felt herself relaxing, enjoying the experience of being a new mother, proud of her baby.

Yet a tiny part of her felt like the impostor she was. She hated that it was a lie. She felt guilty for how happy their assumption had made her feel. Being mistaken for his mother proved that she didn't look totally inept, that she was believable as a parent at least. But the fact remained that she wasn't his real mother, and she could never replace Emily.

The conflict between elation and remorse raged inside her as she pasted on a smile for the women. She could already feel a bond between her and Flynn, the ties of love entwining between her spirit and his, and she knew that it would be devastating for them both if those fragile ribbons were severed.

And as awful as she felt about Emily, Flynn had nobody else. She would never have wished Emily harm, but a thought played on her mind that maybe this was the best thing that could have happened to Flynn. Now he wouldn't grow up on the streets. Now he could live each day warm and fed and safe. He wouldn't have to grow hard, resilient to the terrors of living rough. The streets were no place for a child. And she would give him every drop of love he deserved. He would never be without the love of a mother. It just wouldn't be Emily.

Out of the corner of her eye, she spotted a mannequin displaying a baby sling. She politely excused herself and wound a path over to it. It wasn't the great swathes of material Emily had been wearing, no, this was fixed together with clips and looked more like a backpack. But Flynn was used to being carried close and as soon as she laid eyes on the sling she knew she needed it. She wanted to hold him close and smell his head as he drifted off to sleep, to help him feel safe just as Emily had.

Saraya's heart suddenly thudded unevenly as she realised that the shopkeeper had been gone a long time. Her palms broke out in a sweat as she imagined the worst, and her gaze swung to the road outside the window, looking for evidence of their imminent capture. She instinctively wrapped her arms around Flynn and turned for the door, wide strides carrying her away, the need to protect him from danger vibrating sharply through her.

A door banged from the back of the shop making her jump and turn. The woman emerged with an apologetic smile, wheeling a cheery yellow buggy. "So sorry that took forever, I got a bit stuck out there. I need to get that stockroom organised."

Saraya felt a sharp sting as she bit down hard, and tasted blood on her tongue. She sucked her swollen lip into her mouth, swallowing thickly as the metallic fluid trickled down her throat. Wiping her palms one at a time on her jeans she jiggled Flynn nervously on her hip, hiding her shaking hands under his cardigan.

Taking a measured step back towards the woman, she cleared her throat and appraised the buggy. "Yes, that's just the thing," she said her voice falsely bright. She steadied her hand and turned to point at the sling. "And I'll take one of those too, please."

Chapter Eleven

Saraya pounded the pavement, her cheeks flushed with embarrassment at the glances of passing pedestrians as Flynn railed against her, his screams piercing and furious as he pushed and fought, attacking her chest from his position in the new sling. The moment they had walked through the front door, he had switched from the happy curious baby she had been parading around at the shops, and instead had begun to scream like a child possessed.

Saraya had tried everything. Offering food, toys, books. Changing his nappy. Trying to rock him to sleep. Even putting the television on to try and distract him from his anguish. Nothing worked. He wailed with an intensity that shook Saraya to her core. Her nerves felt frayed, her eardrums felt like swollen sponges, an ache forming deep within them. It had taken an hour of trying to calm him to no avail before she had suddenly realised with a pang of immeasurable sadness, that Flynn was crying simply because he missed his mummy.

Of course he wanted Emily, it was so ridiculously obvious now she thought about it. He had been in shock, confused at what was going on and utterly exhausted, swept from the life he knew and thrown into the arms of a stranger. But now enough was enough. He was with an alien in an unfamiliar world and he was no doubt utterly terrified, craving the safety of familiar, loving arms. He wanted the one thing Saraya couldn't fix for him, no matter how much she wanted to help him feel whole again.

It hurt her deeply to know he was in pain and that no matter how much he cried, it would make no difference. His mother was never coming back. Saraya felt his agony as deeply as if it were her own. She couldn't stop his tears, she couldn't erase his longing and desperation. All she could do was be there for him as he cried his heart out and took his fury out on her. She was amazed at how much stamina he had, how he could keep up the near constant screams without succumbing to exhaustion. It was clearly pure desperation that spurred him onwards.

After two hours though, Saraya had begun to tire.

Every ounce of energy had been squeezed from her, her emotions were raw and shredded as she'd struggled to remain supportive and calm for him. She'd needed to try something else – anything else – if she were to keep her sanity.

So she walked. She walked to distract herself from the incessant shrieks which rattled her deeply. She walked to disperse her stress and the growing frustration she felt at having no solution for this hurting child. She walked because she hoped the fresh air would make Flynn feel better and give him something familiar to hold onto. And finally, she walked because she could see it was working.

After three hours and fifty two minutes of flat out crying, Flynn was starting to fade. His eyes were swollen and red against his pale mottled skin, but she was sure they were beginning to grow heavy. His head dropped to her chest, and he fought it, pushing himself up with an anguished cry. He bobbed unsteadily for a minute or two and then Saraya felt victory at last as he lolled against her and gave in to the bone deep exhaustion. He had given up. His tears had gone unanswered by the person who mattered most.

Saraya felt shaken. Her legs burned with the exertion of walking so hard and so fast, her arms felt like jelly and she realised that she had missed two meals today. Yet, she didn't turn back towards home. She couldn't bear the thought of going through her front door and having it start all over again. And so she walked. And she rejoiced in the silence of a slumbering child, as only a parent can.

Three days passed and Saraya began to wonder if Flynn would ever get over the loss of his mother. Most of his waking hours we're spent crying pitifully and relentlessly, the spaces in between filled with sullen silences and empty eyes. He was hurting dreadfully.

Saraya had called into work to tell them she was taking the holiday she had accrued over the past year. Three weeks, she told them. Not surprisingly, they had refused and told her she needed to book ahead, just like everyone else, and what made her think she was so special anyway? So, she had quit. Just like that. It was amazing how free she'd felt telling them where they could stick their job. It had been fun to hear Anne, her supervisor splutter and cough in disbelief as she had calmly told her that she would not be returning at all, since they wouldn't accommodate her needs.

The elation had been short lived though as Saraya realised she needed a job to pay for the baby who wouldn't stop screaming. She didn't know how she would cope. She was shattered. She had barely washed, eaten or slept for days. And she felt terribly alone.

Tim had left a voice-mail on her phone during one of the more epic screamfests, but Saraya had neglected to return his call. What would she even say? *Please come and help me calm the baby I stole?* Saraya didn't want to face him yet, she wasn't ready to share Flynn and his story with anyone, so she remained reclusive, loneliness permeating her days as she struggled to make things right for Flynn.

On the fourth morning, as the sun was beginning

to stream in watery rays through the window, the situation finally turned a corner. Saraya was sprawled out on a duvet, dozing on the living room floor, a sleeping Flynn beside her. She had paced back and forth for hours before he had succumbed to sleep, the rooms dark and quiet in the dead of night as her cold, bare feet had padded over creaky floorboards.

After a lot of experimentation, this had been the one place he would settle, swaddled tightly in a blanket and tucked between the coffee table and the sofa. It felt like camping at home, and she wondered idly if the cosy space reminded him of places he and Emily had slept in the past.

She stifled a yawn as he began to fidget. Saraya felt dread in the pit of her belly as she awaited the screams that usually came within moments of waking. She didn't know how she would summon the energy to get through another day.

He opened his eyes groggily, slowly focusing on her face. He blinked, then stretched and rolled towards her with a smile, his tongue poking out as he grabbed for her face, patting her cheek with a warm, chubby hand. Hesitantly, she leaned towards him, a smile on her lips.

"Good morning, Flynn," she smiled. He squealed and kicked his legs up and down in delight, grabbing at his feet and trying to bring them to his mouth. Slowly, she leaned down to kiss him softly on the cheek. He responded with a toothy grin.

Encouraged, she kissed him again. He continued to gurgle and smile happily. She took a chance and lowered her head to his round little belly, blowing a playful raspberry against his vest. She lifted her head and grinned in delight as Flynn broke into a fit of giggles. It was the most beautiful sound she had ever heard.

Chapter Twelve

Ten days later

It was possible, Saraya had to admit casting her eyes around the packed room, that Flynn had too many teddy bears. She had lined them up around the room, leaning casually against the sofa and the coffee table and now she was going to get Flynn from the bedroom and surprise him with the teddy bear party. Saraya couldn't believe how excited she was to see his reaction.

She had found herself creating more and more playful games since Flynn had finally begun to settle in with her, and she was constantly surprised at how natural it felt. She had lost nearly an hour playing horsey the day before, bouncing him up and down on her knees, both of them laughing hysterically.

The old Saraya would have rolled her eyes and wondered what the point was and why she wasn't doing something more valuable with her time. But the new Saraya felt like she had been let into a secret world. An hour laughing and bonding with this beautiful baby was the most valuable thing she could possibly do. She didn't consider it a waste in the slightest.

She wandered through the hall and called Flynn's name softly so as not to startle him. He was still very jumpy. Sometimes, when he was babbling loudly and investigating some toy or piece of fluff, his eyes focused and alert in curious exploration, it was easy to forget what he had been through. When she cuddled him now, he no longer felt rigid against her. When she changed his nappy he didn't flinch and scream. But he was far from recovered from his ordeal.

During sleep, he would frequently start suddenly, throwing his limbs out in jerky motions as if he were trying to hold onto something that was slipping from his grasp. If he woke and she was out of the room, even for a second, he would panic.

He didn't give a little tester cry or a gurgle. He would go straight into the most anguished, heart wrenching wail Saraya had ever heard, and it would take twenty minutes or more before she could manage to reassure him and calm him down. Her heart broke for him every time she saw his scared little face, red and tear stained as he clung to her desperately, as if telling her not to leave him again.

And she tried not to, not when he was asleep. She knew it was utterly terrifying for him to drift off in safe, warm arms and wake up alone, and she tried her best to save him from that horror. She knew his need for her was deeply rooted and when he found himself alone, his world crumbled. How could it not after all that had happened?

It was only in the last few days that Saraya had been able to walk around their home and leave him for a few minutes in another room. He had been investigating the wicker laundry basket when she'd left him, and she poked her head around the bedroom door now to find him still there, rubbing his index finger over the rough surface, poking it through the little gaps. His mouth was ajar and a tiny trail of dribble ran from the corner of his lip and down his chin.

As Saraya watched him she felt her heart swell.

Everything about him was so pure. There was a wisdom to the way he explored, his habit of giving each item his full attention for as long as it needed. As she quietly watched him, Saraya wondered when it was that she had lost that single minded focus. Her whole life had been about staying busy, being productive, multi-tasking. Because that is what justifies our place in the world, isn't it? We need to be seen to be achieving, making progress, doing *something*.

But where had it gotten her? She had been miserable. She'd hated her job, and had no passion for what she had spent the majority of her time doing or thinking about. This realisation had been seeping in slowly over the past few days.

If it wasn't for Flynn, she could have easily carried on along the same unending path of monotony until she died. She would have reached the end of her life with thirty thousand wasted days under her belt and never known what it meant to experience something real, or joyful, or precious. Well no more. She was going to follow Flynn's example and stop rushing about doing unnecessary tasks, and instead focus on the pleasures that came with living simply.

She wanted to go outside at dawn and stand barefoot on the grass, feeling each dewy blade between her toes. She wanted to take Flynn on a picnic and make daisy chains, and look at every puff of cloud floating above her. She wanted to take her imagination out of the box she'd locked it up in so long ago, and finally set it free. To find out who she really was deep in her core, because after all these years, she'd realised that she really didn't know herself at all.

Flynn seemed to sense her presence and turned his head towards her with a wide grin. He had four sparkling little teeth in his otherwise gummy mouth and Saraya smiled back, her heart melting at the sight of him.

"Do you want to come and see what I've made for you, Flynn?" she asked softly, holding out her arms towards him. She had made it a rule to never pick him up unless he indicated that he wanted her to. She wanted him to feel he had a choice, and to know that she respected it, even when his answer was no.

He pointed to her with one tiny finger and then shouted joyfully, holding his arms up towards her in assent. She lowered herself down and scooped him up, her eyes meeting his. For a moment, they simply stared at one another, reconnecting without words. Flynn reached forward and patted her cheek, and she kissed him softly on the forehead with a happy sigh.

She walked him through to the living room and placed him gently on the floor where he could see the bears. She sat down quietly on the floor beside him and waited for him to notice them. He had been able to roll and shuffle a little on his bottom when she had brought him home with her, but in the past few days he had looked like he was trying to crawl.

Flynn squealed at a nearby bear and pointed, looking up at Saraya for reassurance. "You can go and see him if you like," she said with a smile. He patted his hands on his knees and squealed again. He shuffled forward a little and grabbed the bear, bringing it to his mouth and sucking on its shiny black nose.

A bright pink hippopotamus from the opposite side of the room caught his attention. He shouted and began to shuffle towards it on his bottom, tossing the bear aside. Halfway across the room, he stopped, spread his legs in a wide V shape, lowered his head and rested it on the rug. Saraya couldn't help but let out a little laugh at the sight of him. He lifted his head and grinned at her, pushing himself up into a crawling position.

Tentatively he rocked back and forth as she had seen him do several times. But this time, instead of giving up, he slowly lifted a hand and leaned forward. His left leg raised and moved a few inches towards the hippo. And then, as if something clicked in his mind, he was off, slowly but surely crawling towards his goal.

Saraya held her breath in excitement. The joy of getting to be the first person to witness this milestone was absolute. She felt ready to burst with pride and adoration. Flynn reached the stuffed toy but didn't stop. He bundled it over and came to rest with his dribbly grin looming over the hippo's enormous head.

He lowered himself down to lay on top of it, his arms wrapped around it in a tight embrace.

Saraya grinned with delight. This was *not* wasted time. She couldn't think of a more valuable way to spend her day. The happiness she felt as she watched his expression of self satisfaction was like nothing she had felt before. In fact, she pondered, she couldn't remember the last time she had felt pure joy prior to meeting Flynn. She was surprised when she considered it, realising how long she had accepted living without such an important emotion.

But now, something had changed within her. She'd had a taste of what life could be like. Of feeling something immense, and strong. Of knowing the power of love and joy and of waking up excited to be alive. She knew that no matter what happened from here on in, she would never accept less than this again. She would never again become the robot she had been just a few weeks before. She couldn't go back.

Chapter Thirteen

Saraya rushed to the living room, grabbing the ringing phone and swiping her finger across the screen before the tone could wake Flynn. She had only just got him settled and her day would be in tatters if he woke up now. She had meant to cut the call off, but Saraya swore under her breath as she realised she had answered it instead. The display read Coralie. She held the phone to her ear and sighed.

"Hi, Sis."

"Saraya! How are you? I haven't heard from you!"

"Sorry, I've been busy. I'm fine."

"Busy? With what? Surely not that boring job of yours?" She gave a tinkling, sickly sweet laugh.

"No, not with work," Saraya said firmly. "With my son." The words left her mouth before Saraya had been sure she was ready to share them, but the moment they were out she knew she didn't want to take them back. She was proud to call Flynn her son, why shouldn't she tell her?

Coralie spluttered. "Your... son?"

"That's right."

"Is this some sort of joke, Saraya? I don't get it."

"Nope. I adopted a baby." Saraya waited, smiling a little as her sister took a moment to process her revelation. She couldn't think of anything that would shock her sister more than this. After all, she had never been able to see Saraya as a mother. Perhaps this would be the catalyst to changing that. It would have to be. "Coralie? Are you still there?"

"Well, yes I'm still here, but what on earth do you expect me to say? How long have you been planning this? Why didn't you tell me? Do Mum and Dad know?"

"I didn't tell anyone. You're the first to call so you're the first one I've told. You know I like to keep things private."

"Well," she choked. "Well... Tim's involved I presume?"

"Uh, no. I'm doing this alone."

"Oh, Saraya. What am I always telling you? Motherhood isn't for everyone, darling, you can't just do it on a whim. It's too hard for that."

Saraya swallowed back her retort denying that it was a whim. It *had* been sudden and unplanned. But that didn't mean it was wrong.

"His name is Flynn. He's ten months old," she said proudly, though her sister hadn't asked. "I love him. And you will too," she told her, though she was doubtful it was true. Sometimes it didn't look as though Coralie even loved her own children, though Saraya was hopeful she did behind closed doors at least.

Coralie sighed. "I wish you had told me what you were planning, Saraya. I could have..."

"What? Talked me out of it?"

"Helped you to... see sense."

"I thought – " Saraya paused, only now realising what she had secretly hoped for. That her sister would finally see her as a woman rather than a silly child. That she would be proud of her, include her in her life, talk to her openly, mother to mother. But Saraya realised now with a sinking heart that it was never going to happen. To Coralie, Saraya would always be a silly, irresponsible girl. The annoying seven year old her parents had adopted and forced her to endure. Coralie had enjoyed the novelty of having a sister to begin with, but it hadn't taken long before she'd lost interest in her new pet and treated her as nothing more than an irritation she longed to be rid of. No matter what Saraya did, no matter how much she achieved, Coralie would always find a way to twist it and make her look the fool.

"You thought what?" Coralie pushed, her tone cold.

"It doesn't matter. Look, Cora, I've got to go."

"Go on then. Back to playing mummies and daddies. Oh wait. Just mummies, isn't it?" she said nastily. Saraya swallowed and bit her lip angrily. She counted to five in her head. "Bye, Coralie," she forced out into the mouthpiece. She ended the call without waiting to hear any more and switched the phone off, tossing it onto the sofa.

She felt strangely calm. It certainly wasn't the first time that Coralie had tried to make her feel like an idiot, and if she was honest with herself, in the past it had usually worked. Coralie had a way of finding the spot that was most sensitive and grating away at it until she was left in shreds. Time and time again, Saraya had been reduced to tears from feeling so utterly rejected by her older sister.

But this time was different. It didn't matter. Coralie could be happy for her, or she could be bitter and judgemental. It was a shame, but it didn't feel like all the other times. Saraya wasn't alone in this. She didn't need her sister's approval to be a mother. She didn't need a bunch of strangers and a stack of paperwork telling her what she already knew. That she *was* a mother. She just needed one person to agree with her, and she knew he did.

She padded into the bedroom and leaned over the Moses basket, marvelling at the soft sweetness of the dark haired baby sleeping inside. Her heart felt ready to burst as she watched his chest slowly rise and fall. She was his. And Cora could disapprove and roll her eyes and tell her she couldn't manage alone, but it didn't matter. It was too late. Their hearts were already too entangled to ever untie.

Flynn snuffled in his sleep and fluttered his bleary

eyes. Saraya felt her arms move towards him, needing to hold him against her and keep him safe. She lifted him to her chest and he looked up at her through heavy lids. Sleepily, he gripped the fabric of her dress in his soft little fist, and pursed his lips. She watched him, every second a precious gift. "Ma," he said, his eyes on hers. "Mama." He smiled and then curled into her warmth, letting sleep take him again. Saraya's heart pounded. One little word. *Mama*. She had never been called anything so wonderful in her whole life. He was hers, she was his. With that one sweet word, he gave her all the approval she would ever need.

Chapter Fourteen

Five hundred and thirty-three days. That's the average length of time it takes between a child being placed in care and them going home with their adoptive family. Five hundred and thirty three. That's one year and five months. 12792 hours. 767,520 minutes. Saraya had read all the figures, memorised all the facts as she'd tried to make sense of her childhood.

She had envied those children when she'd first read that number. Her time in the system had been far longer. For the first five years she had been yo-yoed between her biological parents and foster care. Always a different family. Always a new, uncertain start. She could still remember the sheer terror she had felt, searching for a familiar face, finding nobody she recognised.

Months would pass. Her parents would visit and they would promise her she could come home soon. And after what seemed like an eternity, their promises would come true. Those were the best times. When they were determined to be the parents they said she deserved. When her family began to pass for normal. They would all cuddle up together in bed in the early hours of the morning, tickling each other and sharing their dreams. She had held hands with her mother as they'd walked to the beach, laughed as they chased each other and built sandcastles.

Her father had made her the best dens imaginable. Rainbow coloured teepees constructed of old holey sheets and upturned furniture. One time, they had pulled her bed covers into the cosy darkness and he'd told her stories long into the night, his deep, soothing voice lulling her to sleep in his safe, strong arms.

But it had never lasted. As much as they wanted to get it right, as much as they loved Saraya, they both had a stronger, darker love for something else. Heroin. As time passed, they would grow more and more irritable. They would begin to pull away. Saraya could feel it happening, but she could never seem to stop it. She was never enough to keep them grounded.

They would drift into their world, the one where

she wasn't invited, and she would find herself scrounging for her dinner, wandering aimlessly around their dark, dirty home, waiting for someone to wake up and play. Her mother had held her so close, weeping with shame when they took her away that last time. They had both known that this time it would be forever.

Saraya had been found standing on the pavement at eleven p.m. asking for help from passing strangers. She had only tried to cook an egg. It seemed easy enough to do, and she had been so very hungry. She'd watched her mother doing it so many times before. But the egg was slippery and hard to crack. It had fallen from her tiny hands, its sticky yellow contents spilling across the plate. Saraya had reached out and grabbed a tea towel to wipe the mess, but in her haste, she had dragged it through the open flame of the hob, setting it alight. Dropping it to the ground, she had rushed to wake her parents, but they were unresponsive. "Utterly irresponsible and selfish," the judge had labelled them, according to the paperwork Saraya had requested when she'd turned eighteen.

She had been placed with a foster family just three months after her fifth birthday. During the two years that followed, she'd been moved a further four times. "Unforeseen circumstances," they had said. "Change of plans."

Saraya had seen first hand how children like her were dragged from pillar to post, with no thought for their emotional needs. It didn't matter that the families were kind to her. What difference could it make? How could she possibly relax and learn to trust them, when she knew that tomorrow she could be ripped out of that life and expected to start from scratch all over again? Those two years had been awful. She'd shut herself down, numbed herself to her reality, just wishing and dreaming of the day that she would finally have a proper family. Hope was the only thing that got her through the unbearable loneliness.

When at last she was chosen by a family, she thought she would burst with joy. The time had finally come for her to be held close and loved and wanted beyond reason. She could not stop grinning as she'd waited beside her packed bags, ready to be collected by her new family. That feeling had lasted for exactly one day. After arriving at their house, it quickly became apparent that these people were not the parents of her dreams. They hadn't been waiting desperately for her to come home. They didn't care to hear about her past, her interests, her thoughts or her fears. She was to be a companion child. A playmate for their lonely, only daughter. Never an equal. Never to be showered in the love her adoptive sister received.

Saraya knew exactly how it felt to not have one single person in your life you can rely on. She knew what it was like to wake up not knowing whether today you would be moved away to another strange place, with another unfamiliar face smiling down at you.

She had no need to imagine the world she was striving to protect Flynn from. She *knew*. She wouldn't give him up to see him become just another lost child. He was loved and she was never going to give him a chance to doubt that.

Saraya was just placing Flynn into the Moses basket beside her bed when the doorbell rang. "Shit," she whispered. It would no doubt be Derek, the postman with that set of wooden farm animals she'd ordered. She watched Flynn for signs of waking. He sighed, turned onto his side and continued to sleep. Quickly, before he rang the bell again, she stole out of the bedroom and pulled the door, leaving it slightly ajar so she would hear if he woke.

She tiptoed to the front door and flung it open, ready to give him a piece of her mind about inconsiderate noise.

"Hi."

"Oh, Tim. I thought you were... nevermind. Hi."

"I've been waiting for your call. It never came," Tim shrugged, leaning against the door frame. "I wanted to check you were alright... that *we* were alright," he paused. "Are you?"

"Yes, sorry. I know I should have called but some things came up and I guess time just got away from me. I'm sorry."

"But you're okay?" Tim pressed.

"Yes. I'm fine."

"Good. So can I come in?"

"Uh…"

"Oh come on Saraya, I don't understand these games you're playing. I just want to come in for a coffee and hear what's been going on. If you don't want me here just tell me straight and I'll go, but I'm struggling to understand why you're avoiding me. What's the big problem?"

"Nothing. There's no problem." Saraya hesitated, then pulled open the door. Tim shook his head with a frown and then strode past her and into the kitchen. He looked around at the mess.

"What's been going on here? Are you ill?" he asked, sweeping his arm to indicate the piles of unwashed plates in the sink, the dirty laundry stacked on the floor beside the washing machine.

"No, not ill. Just busy." She filled the kettle and busied herself with finding two clean cups. He was right of course, she had let the place go a bit, and she was normally so on top of things, he was bound to notice the change. But Flynn took a lot more time than she had expected, and in the moments when he slept and she should probably have been cleaning, she usually ended up hypnotised by the slow rise and fall of his little chest or even better, falling asleep beside his warm little body, curling up with him on the bed.

She was too exhausted to do much more than that, and honestly, she hated tearing herself away from him to do mundane tasks. Thinking of how lovely a nap would be right now, she stifled a yawn.

Tim scrutinised her and rubbed his hand over the blonde stubble on his chin. "Something's different. What's going on, Saraya?"

She opened the fridge, pulling out a carton of milk and gripping it between her hands. "I've been thinking about what we talked about. About finding my purpose. I think I've found it. In fact, I'm certain I have."

"Really?" Tim lit up. "That's excellent news. I wasn't expecting you to move so fast." He pushed a stack of unopened post aside and leaned his elbows on the workbench. "So tell me then."

She poured the coffee slowly, unsure how much

she should say. Could she trust him to keep her secret? He had always been there for her, but this was bigger than anything she had ever shared, was it too much to expect him to understand? Just then Flynn let out a wail. Saraya's eyes flashed towards the bedroom. "Was that... a baby?" Tim asked, wide eyed.

"Um, yes... Wait here, I'll just go and get him." She left Tim standing alone as she rushed off to scoop up the precious bundle. Soothing him against her chest, she came back into the kitchen. "Tim," she smiled proudly. "I'd like you to meet Flynn. My son."

Saraya yawned. For three hours she had been explaining the long and horrific story of how Flynn had come to be hers to Tim, and she felt as if they were going around in circles.

"I don't understand how you can do this, Saraya," Tim was saying in exasperation. "It's not right."

"You were the one who kept talking about purpose, Tim. And you were right. My life was empty, meaningless. Until I found Flynn. Now I have a purpose and it's him. I love him. This is it."

"What! Stealing babies? That's your purpose?"

"Oh come on, Tim! You make it sound like I was to blame for what happened. Like I was the one holding the knife!"

"I'm beginning to think anything is possible with you!"

"You seriously think I would hurt someone? Kill a mother and steal her baby? Do you really think that of me, Tim? *Do you?*"

He sighed. "No, Saraya, no of course I don't think that. But you can't keep him. He's not yours."

"Why? Why can't he be mine? He has no one else and his mother is dead. If I give him to the police, he could end up with anyone. Isn't it better that he is with someone who really loves him, who really wants him?" she implored. "So what that we didn't do the paperwork? This baby would have ended up going from foster home to foster home and you know it. I won't do that to him. He's mine." She tightened her grip around the baby, who was busily banging a stuffed rabbit against her cheek. "He's been through too much already. I won't make him lose me too."

"It's not your choice to make. You can't just keep a baby you found in the street, Saraya, that's not how the world works. And you just left his mother there. Why didn't you call the police?"

"Oh we've been through this!" Saraya cried in exasperation. "I told you, it was too late. She was dead, there was no way to save her. But they would have taken Flynn and I couldn't let that happen. They already found Emily, it was in the newspaper the day after she died. Look." She reached under the coffee table and pulled out the paper, turning the pages until she located the story she was looking for.

A homeless woman estimated to be in her mid thirties was found dead in an underground bypass in Oxford Circus in the early hours of Saturday morning. Her throat had been slit. Police suspect the murder was drugs related but as yet they have no leads. The woman had no identification or personal belongings. Anyone with any information should contact the 24 hour police hotline on 0800 555 999.

"See? They aren't even looking for him. They don't even know she had a baby. And it's been three weeks, nobody has come forward. She had no one," Saraya said sadly. "Flynn has nowhere else to go."

"That's really not the point though, is it?"

"Tim, please. I *need* this. I need him. It's too late to change my mind, I can't give him up. Please, just understand, can't you?"

"But how can you love him so soon and so strong? I don't get it."

Saraya ran her fingers through Flynn's fine hair, a smile forming on her lips. "Love isn't something you can control or explain. It emerges from your soul and takes over your heart. I felt it the moment I held him in my arms and it has grown stronger every day since. Even when I feel like I love him more than I can bear, it continues to grow."

She leaned forward and brushed a kiss over the baby's downy forehead. Then she lifted her face meeting Tim's eyes with her own. "The love of a mother for her child has no limit. It expands farther than the reaches of the universe. It is the most dangerous and wonderful feeling I have ever known."

"Dangerous?" Tim repeated, his voice cautious. "Dangerous how?"

"Because there is nothing I wouldn't do to keep him from harm, Tim. *Nothing*. I used to have the ability to reason, to water down my reactions for the sake of being polite or minding someone's feelings. Not anymore. I can feel it, this new depth to my capabilities. It's reckless but it's undeniable. I mean it when I say I would do anything. It must be the oldest instinct in the world, that of a mother protecting her child. I feel as though a grizzly bear wouldn't have a chance against me if he tried to take him from me." She looked at Tim, a fierce glint in her eyes challenging him to make her prove it.

"The law doesn't mean a thing to me now. It makes things black and white and misses the rainbow in between. They would take him from me in a second, rip him from my arms, with no thought for his feelings, or mine. And all in the name of blindly following some legislation that a bunch of people we've never even met, voted on once upon a time." She leaned forward, her eyes burning into his.

"Tim, please, I need you to understand, I'm doing this because it's right for Flynn. I would give him up in a second if I thought it was best for him, but I don't. Please just understand that."

"Saraya, look at what you're asking me to do!" Tim shook his head in exasperation. He got to his feet and paced towards the window, running his fingers back and forth over his lips. "For fuck sake, Saraya," he said quietly. "What is my job? What do I do for a living?"

Saraya's blood turned to ice. "Tim, no," she whispered in horror. "Please."

"I have a duty of care. Do you know what that means?" he asked, turning to face her. "I can't keep this secret for you, Saraya, I can't. That baby needs to be assessed, properly, by people who know what they're doing. Social services. *Me*. You can't hide him forever, Saraya and people are going to want to know how you came to have a six month old baby in your home. How do you plan to explain that?"

Saraya didn't bother to correct his mistake over Flynn's age. "I'll just tell everyone I adopted him. Why couldn't I have?"

"You didn't though! That might work for your

work colleagues, but the police will know within an hour that you're lying."

"But the police won't look. They don't know me. I'm not a suspect and there's no evidence to tie me to the crime."

"You don't know that! Oh come on, Saraya, this isn't the dark ages. There is technology you wouldn't believe, cameras everywhere. They might still find you."

Saraya shook her head wearily. "They won't."

"They might. And then what, you're in the shit because you didn't come forward. And I lose everything because I didn't turn you in."

"It won't come to that," Saraya pouted stubbornly. "Tim, I won't give him up. He needs me more than you could possibly understand. And I need him. Please Tim. I know I'm asking something huge from you, but please, just don't report us. If it all comes crashing down I promise I won't mention your name. You won't get dragged down with me. Please, just consider it, won't you?"

Tim ran his fingers through his hair and brought

his palm to rest over his mouth, his thumb rubbing in angry strokes across his cheekbone. His nostrils flared as he breathed in deeply. Saraya watched him nervously, her grip tightening around Flynn as she waited for him to speak.

"I can't make you any promises, but I'll consider it. That's all I can offer. But this is the end for us, Saraya, I won't be a part of this. I'm not going to play happy families with a stolen baby."

"I understand," Saraya breathed, her shoulders slumping in relief. "Thank you, Tim. I know this isn't what you expected, but thank you. He *is* cared for, you don't need to worry about that."

"That's not what I'm worrying about," he said gruffly. He took a step towards her, leaning forward to brush a kiss across her cheek. He touched a finger to the baby's tiny nose, and shook his head, swallowing back words that were too painful to say. "I'll call you," he muttered, turning to pick up his jacket and walking out.

Saraya listened for the click of the front door and startled herself with a giddy laugh. She was surprised to feel hot tears falling heavily down her cheeks as the nerves rolled over her. She'd come close to having to really fight for him then, too damn close and though she'd kept her cool, she had never been so scared in her life, not even when she had found Emily.

She felt primal, a lioness protecting her cub, more powerful than she'd ever known she could be. If Tim wanted to fight, she would be ready. *I dare you,* she thought, *I fucking dare you.*

Chapter Fifteen

She needed a back up plan. Flynn's safety rested entirely on the whim of a disgruntled, now ex, boyfriend. Saraya thought carefully, trying to second guess what Tim would do. The truth was, even after all this time she still didn't know him well enough to be sure. He could turn her in tomorrow and then everything would fall to pieces. She wouldn't let that happen.

But what she was considering now was frightening. She had promised herself that she wouldn't call *her* again, especially after the last time. Saraya shivered remembering it. Her best friend, the girl she had played Barbies with as a child and who had taught her how to French plait her hair so it curled when she took it down, the one who had covered for her when she was late to school, who had slapped Johnny Richards hard across his face when he had cheated on Saraya with Lottie North in year eleven. *Natalia*.

Natalia, who had gone down a very different path from Saraya as soon as school was over. Who had started selling cocaine and god knows what else, "Because it's just so lucrative, Saraya!" Natalia who had married Hex, the biggest dealer in the country and had laughed as the millions came rolling in. The woman who had come to Christmas at Saraya's parents house with her junkie friend Mary, who had stolen her Dad's brand new laptop along with half the other presents. Natalia, who had taken Saraya to a party and laughed as some lecherous old perv had fawned over her, and promised her he would make it worth her while as he tried to rip open her blouse. Saraya shuddered. *Fucking Natalia.* Of course she would be the only person who could help her now.

It was a friendship that refused to die. Over the years, as Natalia had gone further and further down the path of crime and danger, Saraya had found herself becoming more and more serious. But as hard as she'd tried, she had never been able to cut ties with her rebellious friend. Their bond went too deep. So rather than walk away, Saraya had tried to balance out the harsh side of her, by refusing anything that could be considered risky or adventurous. Always choosing the sensible option.

She'd been the steady, reliable, and quite frankly up until this past month, boring one, in an attempt to be a good influence on her friend. It hadn't worked. It had taken a long time for Saraya to realise that the only person she could control in life, was herself. She'd had no choice but to accept Natalia just the way she was and to give up on trying to change her.

After Natalia decided to leave England and their friendship became more intermittent, Saraya had found that her habits had become too ingrained to let go of. She was too used to saying no, to walking the conventional path, to be able to break away and shake herself out of her safe little bubble. But not anymore.

Saraya drummed her fingernails restlessly on her knee. "Oh well, looks like I'm going to have to suck it up and call the bitch," she muttered, reaching for the phone. The last number she had for her was for her mansion in Majorca. It had been nearly two years since they had spoken to each other. She hoped she was still there.

The phone rang once, twice, three times and

Saraya was just considering chickening out when someone picked up. "Hello?" came a sleep muffled voice.

"Is that Natalia? It's Saraya..."

"Saraya! You're joking. How are you, babe? It's been ages."

"I know, yeah, I'm okay. Just been busy, you know?"

"Yeah, me too, you know how it is," she laughed.

Saraya frowned, not wanting to think about whatever it was she was up to that was keeping her so busy. "Look, Nat, I hate to call you after so long and ask for a favour, but I really need one. A big one."

"Okaaaay," she answered cautiously. "So what is it?"

"I don't really want to say over the phone. Is there any chance you're coming to London any time soon? Like really soon?"

"Well, I wasn't planning on it, but I think I probably owe you one after Aiden's party, don't I? Richard's not great with the ladies, is he?" she giggled.

"No. He's not," she replied icily. Natalia was silent.

"But don't worry about it, these things happen," Saraya said hurriedly, trying to keep things friendly. She didn't want to piss off the one person who could save her. "So could you come? Today?"

"Today?" Natalia repeated in surprise? "What's the big hurry? Oh I know, I know, you don't want to tell me over the phone. *Fine*. I need to do some shopping anyway, it's rubbish over here. I'll see what I can do and get back to you, okay?"

"Yes. Thank you," Saraya breathed.

"No problem, what are friends for?" Natalia chirped. "Can't wait to hear the big mystery. Mwah!" The line went dead and Saraya stared down at the black haired baby in her arms, wondering if she had done the right thing.

Twenty minutes later her phone beeped with a text message.

Okay Chica, we're on. Meet me @ 10.30pm, usual place. Mines a vodka tonic. Big kiss! xx

Saraya stared at the message until her eyes blurred, amazed at what she was willing to do for her child.

Chapter Sixteen

Saraya pushed the buggy over the narrow cobbled street, a cosy Flynn tucked up warm inside, thankfully sleeping soundly. She hated dragging him out in the cold at this time, but since she had nobody she could trust to look after him, this was her only option.

She rounded a corner and saw the faded hanging sign of Giuseppe's Italian restaurant. It swung gently back and forth on the breeze, an eerie squeak emitting as it grated against the rusty hinges. The windows were dark, but Saraya knew they were misleading. She pushed the buggy ahead and stopped in front of the filthy wooden door, hesitating as she argued back and forth with herself.

She didn't want to bring Flynn inside, to take him into that world. She wanted to run home and get back into bed with her baby and stay there forever. But she knew that she would never feel safe there until she did this. It was with Flynn's safety in mind that she placed her hand on the smooth brass handle and pushed open the door, flooding the cobbles with light.

She hoisted the buggy over the threshold and was transported back in time, or so it felt. Nothing had changed. The same round pine tables, their surfaces scratched and worn. The chairs with the cracked burgundy PVC padded seats. The wine bottle candle holders, wax dripping in rivulets forming hot puddles at their bases. The low voices as deals were made, hand shakes in dark corners. And there he was, the man himself. Giuseppe.

He was bustling through the restaurant, a glass of red in one hand, clapping diners heartily on the shoulder and jovially pouring wine into already full glasses with the other. Saraya had always liked Giuseppe, in spite of herself. He knew what went on among his patrons, and turned a blind eye to all of it, though there were deals made that would destroy lives and hurt innocent people.

In Saraya's mind, he was as guilty as the criminals that frequented his premises simply because he didn't ever turn anyone in, no matter what their crime. But he had always been kind to her and treated her with love and it was hard not to like the man, though she wished she didn't. And for once she was glad of his discretion. She didn't want her secrets getting out.

Just then Giuseppe looked up and saw Saraya. He beamed, throwing his hands into the air as he made a beeline for her. "Mio dio! My beautiful Saraya! How long it has been you naughty girl!" he bellowed, engulfing her in a hug that left her gasping for breath. "And I see you've been busy," he winked, peering into the buggy at the now wide eyed Flynn. The baby took one look at the enormous bear of a man looming over him and broke into an ear splitting scream.

"Good lungs. A healthy boy!" Giuseppe announced with pride, as Saraya fumbled with the straps and lifted him into her arms.

"Thank you," she smiled. "It's good to see you too, Giuseppe. How have you been?"

"Busy, merry and drunk mostly," he boomed. "Nothing as productive as you. You look well, mio caro. Motherhood suits you."

Saraya smiled and bowed her head. "I'm glad you think so. It's hard work but I wouldn't trade it for the world." She soothed Flynn, rubbing circles on his back as he peered over her shoulder, looking intently at the flickering candles and animated diners. It was obvious that he wouldn't be going back to sleep any time soon.

"Let me take that for you and put it out the back," Giuseppe smiled, his large hand reaching out and grasping hold of the buggy. Saraya tried to object but he was already shoving his way between the tables, striking up a conversation with a group of women dressed scantily in leather and lace. She decided to let him go.

She scanned the room and found Natalia staring at her, her over coloured brows arched inquiringly, a cigarette drooping from glossy pink lips. Weaving her way through the restaurant to her friend, with Flynn making attempts to grab anything within reaching distance, she finally made it over to the corner where Natalia was sitting. "Hi."

"You have a baby."

"Yes."

"Please, please tell me that this favour doesn't involve me looking after this baby. You know I don't do children."

Saraya smiled. "Don't panic. I'm not going to ask you to look after my baby, okay? You can relax. But put out that cigarette, I don't want him breathing in that stuff."

Natalia regarded her with narrowed eyes. She took a deep drag, turned her head and blew away from Flynn. With a long fuchsia nail she pulled the thick glass ashtray towards her and stubbed out the rest with a shake of her head. "There, happy?" she asked.

"Yes. Thanks." Saraya pulled out a chair and sat, giving Flynn a sticky laminated menu to play with. He whacked it against her ear and she ignored him.

Natalia watched him with an air of disgust. "When did you have a baby, Saraya? I can't believe you didn't tell me about this before."

"There hasn't been much time to tell you anything. I've only had him a few weeks."

"So he's not really yours?"

"Yes, he is. His mother died and I took him. I don't want to go into the details, but..."

"You didn't bother with the paperwork?" Natalia

guessed astutely.

Saraya looked her in the eye, pursing her lips tightly. Finally, she answered. "No, Nat, I didn't. And I won't. They'll take him from me if they find out I have him and I won't let that happen."

Natalia gave a long low whistle. "Are you sure you really want him, Ray? I mean, you're not exactly Miss Mother Earth. You never wanted one before. Why now?"

"I don't want *"a baby."* I want *this* baby. His name is Flynn. I can't explain why, I just do."

"A baby is one thing, darlin', but he's going to grow. He'll need potty training, he'll be walking around in a year and getting into everything. He'll be a bloody teenager one day. Are you really up for that, Ray? It will be horrendous!"

"Not to me. I'm not stupid, Nat, I know it's going to be hard, but I need to do this. I can't explain how much this little boy is a part of me, he's mine."

"But he's not. You're not his real mum, are you? She's dead. Gone."

Saraya shook her head. "What makes a mother? Is

it blood? Is it a piece of paper saying so? Or is it the fact that for every moment since this baby came into my life, I've put his needs first? I would fight until my body was torn limb from limb, I would cross oceans and give up every single thing I own if it would keep him safe and happy. Doesn't that give me the right to call myself a mother?"

Natalia was silent as she lifted her glass to her lips and sipped the blood red wine thoughtfully. "I guess you're right," she considered, placing her glass back down. "I know too many real mothers who don't go to half those lengths for their kids. Mine included. She couldn't care less about me."

Saraya placed a hand on top of hers, squeezing gently. "I'm sure she cares about you. She just isn't very good at showing it."

"Maybe once, but not any more. Her only concern is herself. But what do I care? I get to live in a mansion in the sun, and she's still whoring it out to anyone who will take her, on that grotty estate. I tried to get her to come out to us, to live or even for a visit, and you know what she said?"

Saraya shook her head sympathetically. "No, what?"

"She told me I was too big for my boots and where did I get off flashing my cash and treating her like a charity case. She pushed me out the door, literally pushed me," Natalia exclaimed in disgust. "And when I tripped backwards and fell in the dirt she just stood there laughing and said, *'looks like you're not so high and mighty now, don't it?'* the cow," Natalia said with a grimace. She rarely spoke about her mum, but I knew how deep the hurt ran inside her.

"I'm sorry."

"Doesn't matter. She's not worth my tears is she? Let her be miserable and alone. All I'm saying is, yes, you're right. Being a good mum isn't necessarily anything to do with blood. If you're willing to be there for this bubba, then who's anyone to say you can't?"

"Thank you. So will you help me?"

She flashed me a smile. "What do you want me to do?"

"I need a way out. I don't know if we'll need to use

it, but if anyone comes snooping around asking questions, I don't want to hang around. I won't take the risk. I need passports, for both of us. New names. And a bank account. Can you sort it?"

"I know the people who can. But it will cost you, these things don't come cheap, Ray."

"I know. I need them to be good though, the last thing I want is to be caught at customs. Can you guarantee they will look the part?"

"They will."

"How soon can you get them? A few days?"

"It will be a week at least, maybe ten days. I'll sort it. Just keep a low profile until then and don't answer the door unless you're sure who it is."

Saraya nodded. "I won't." She slid an envelope across the table to Natalia. "Passport photos. And the date of birth I want Flynn to have." Natalia nodded and slipped the envelope into her bag. She watched as Flynn made a grab for the ashtray and Saraya passed him the pepper mill instead.

"I never would have thought it, but you're good at this, Ray. Motherhood suits you."

Chapter Seventeen

One week later

The park had been icy and brisk, but Saraya had not stopped laughing as Flynn babbled and smiled in the swing. Now she was dawdling along the pavement as they made their way home, playing peek-a-boo with him strapped to her chest in the sling.

She hid her eyes, unable to resist peeking through her fingers at the grinning, dribbly baby, and then when she couldn't bear to wait a single second longer, she threw her hands up shouting "Peek-a-boo," and watching in delight as Flynn fell into ecstatic peals of laughter.

His laugh could thaw even the frostiest of hearts, she thought, as he smiled up at her hoping for more. She covered her eyes again and repeated the game. She couldn't get over the look of joyous surprise on his face every time she reappeared. She played with his little hands and began singing *Row, row, row the boat*, one of his favourites. He loved when she swayed him from side to side in the sling.

Saraya knew she must look ridiculous as she sang and danced her way down the street, but she didn't care one bit. Flynn was content and that made her happier than she'd ever been. She reached her gate and opened it, taking one step along the path before she stopped dead in her tracks. There at her front door were two police officers looking grim.

"Saraya Matthews?" One of them stepped forward, flashing his badge at her.

"Yes."

"I'm Officer Harrison. This is PC Collins. We would like to ask you some questions about a case we're working on. We think you may be able to assist us."

Saraya instinctively stepped back as the officer peered down at the baby. "Really?" she asked, somehow managing to keep her tone casual, though her heart was racing, the moisture evaporating instantly from her mouth. "I can't think how," she smiled, "but of course I'll do what I can. Come inside."

"No, I don't think so, Miss Matthews. I'd rather we talk at the station."

Saraya shook her head, her blood turning to ice in her veins. "That's not really convenient for me. My son is due his nap and he'll get grumpy if we miss it," she said firmly. She wrapped her arms protectively across the baby, tucking her sweating hands beneath them.

"I don't think I made myself clear, I apologise if I made it sound like an option. We need you to come to the station. Now."

"Fine. I'll just grab his bottle and I'll follow you down."

"We'll wait. You can come with us."

"In the police car?"

"Yes."

Saraya shook her head. "No, Fl – my son needs his car seat. I can't do that."

"Don't worry, I'm a safe driver," PC Collins piped up.

"Surely you aren't suggesting that you are somehow immune from having accidents, Constable?

I won't put him at risk."

"Fine, you can put his car seat in our car then," Officer Harrison said firmly. "Go and get what you need, Miss Matthews. Quickly."

Saraya's hands shook as she unlocked her front door and went inside, pushing it shut behind her. She felt tears prick at her eyes and fought them back as she grabbed Flynn's bottle and a sachet of purée for him. Had Tim broken his promise? Had he given her up? Or did they have evidence to link her to Emily? It was too soon. Natalia had said she would deliver the passports this evening. Why did they have to come today?

"Oh god," Saraya whispered, terror flooding through her, her heart skipping erratically as she looked down at Flynn. "What shall I do, baby, what shall I do?" She looked at the window, wondering if she could make it far enough away if she escaped now. A loud banging from the front door jolted her from her thoughts. It would never work. She wouldn't get past the end of the road, and then they would know she was guilty. "Oh, Flynn, I don't know what to do," she whispered desperately.

The banging came again and Saraya knew she had no time. "Hurry up, Miss Matthews," came the deep voice of the first officer. *Officer Harrison,* she thought bleakly. *Maybe they don't know anything. I'll just be helpful and polite and they'll let me go.* She couldn't bear to consider the alternative. Her senses were dull as she put the bottle and food into her bag and walked to the front door.

"Took your time," PC Collins said gruffly.

"I'm sorry, you know babies, they don't travel light," Saraya smiled, her voice falsely bright. "I'll just grab that car seat then." She walked past them and crossed the road to where her Fiat was parked. The two of them stood outside her gate, waiting impatiently.

Saraya leaned into the back of the car, Flynn dangling backwards as she unbuckled the seat, taking as much time as she could get away with. Glancing discreetly at the ignition, she wondered recklessly if she could get the keys in it and get away before they could catch her.

Flynn smiled up at her grabbing her hair as it fell onto his face. *So innocent,* she thought sadly. *He has no idea the danger we're in. I can't let them take him from me, I won't.*

She moved the keys in her palm, readying the right one. Taking a deep breath, she stepped backwards fast, her leg colliding with something hard. Officer Harrison.

"Let me help you with that," he said, leaning into the car and taking the seat. "You seem to be struggling." He stood up straight and waited, a hard expression sweeping across his face.

Well that was that then. She had no choice but to go with them to the station. She pushed the door shut and locked the car, tossing the keys into her bag and reluctantly following him back to the squad car.

As she settled herself in the back beside Flynn, trying to keep her breathing calm, she felt her palms split open as her fingernails dug their way through the soft skin. She was trapped. Every instinct in her body told her to run, to fight, but it would do no good. Her only chance was to cooperate and keep her cool. She had to convince them to let her go. She had to keep Flynn safe. She just had to. The alternative was too awful to even consider.

Chapter Eighteen

Saraya sat on the cold hard plastic chair in the waiting room, shivering with fear as she strained her ears for sounds of approaching footsteps. On arrival to the police station, she and Flynn had been led to the stark room and left completely alone. The officers expressions had been grim as she'd been shepherded in. They had not responded to her nervous chatter.

Twenty minutes had passed, if not thirty, every second creating more tension and turmoil within her frenzied mind. Flynn, thankfully was relaxed and unaware of what was happening. She kissed him softly, a sense of imminent danger pulsing through her veins. *They are going to try and take him.*

She had already peeked outside the door once, only to be greeted by a fierce looking officer at the desk, who had pointedly asked Saraya what she needed, and watched with eagle eyes until she had retreated back inside the room. No window, no posters or artwork, just four cold, bare walls surrounded her. It was as if she were already a prisoner. There was certainly no escape from here. She unfolded a blanket from her bag and placed it on the floor, lowering Flynn down to it. He squealed in delight and kicked his legs, grabbing at his toes. She watched him roll and wriggle across the woollen throw, discovering the world around him.

The door creaked open and there stood PC Collins. Saraya jumped to her feet. "What's going on?" she asked him. "Why are we in here?"

"We're just waiting for someone to come for the baby," he replied.

"What do you mean? *Who?*"

"Someone from social services."

"No," she almost shouted. She took a deep breath, trying to calm her voice. "No," she said firmly. "He stays with me."

"Don't panic, love. It's just while we talk. You can't have him with you while we're questioning you."

"Questioning me? About what?" she demanded. "I don't know what you want from me but I am not going to be separated from my son! You can't take him."

PC Collins regarded her with beady eyes, his sneer sending shivers of hatred through her body. "*Your* son?" he repeated. "Sure about that are you?" He smirked as her jaw dropped, and walked out of the room, closing the door behind him. She stood rooted to the ground, her legs feeling as if someone had poured concrete into them as fear paralysed her.

Flynn giggled and watched her from his spot on the floor. She pasted a smile onto her face and swept him into her arms, pulling him close to her chest. "It's going to be alright, baby. It's got to be." He yawned against her chest and raised a hand to pull on his ear. "Tired, sweetie?" she asked quietly. "Me too."

She sat down with her back to the door and began to hum a tune, watching his eyes begin to grow heavy, slowly closing as he drifted off. She was suddenly aware of voices coming from outside the room. Her whole body became rigid as she waited in terror. Was this it? Had her time come? She wasn't ready.

Saraya wrapped her arms tighter around Flynn, squeezing her eyes shut as she let the sweet baby smell of his head fill her nostrils. Her heart was racing as the voices became louder, their footsteps heavy as they approached. Her hands shook, but her voice was steady as she whispered a lullaby into his downy pink ear.

I won't let them take him, I won't let them take him, she thought over and over again. She rocked back and forth in her seat, trying to soothe herself as much as the baby. Her stomach muscles felt as if they had suffered an iron punch, her breathing became shallow as she swallowed an excess of saliva, praying she wouldn't vomit all over the tiled floor. The door creaked open and several pairs of feet stomped into the room, coming to stop before her.

"Miss?"

The male voice spoke gently, a hand reaching out to touch her shoulder. Saraya ignored him, continuing to hold and rock and sing, her eyes screwed tightly shut. She knew she must appear unhinged, but her arms wouldn't – no, *couldn't* – do it. She couldn't let them take her baby.

As if he could sense her desperation, the bundle in her arms began to whimper. His arms and legs jerked out angrily as he fidgeted and then thrashed against her. Her breath caught in her chest as she tried to placate him, his sobs coming harder, as if *finally* he understood what was coming.

"Miss," the voice came again. "There's no need to panic. I just need to take the baby for a little while, while you speak to these gentlemen. He will be well looked after, I promise."

"No," she spat through gritted teeth. "You can't have him."

She heard a collective sigh from the group and another pair of heavy boots step forward. "Miss Matthews," came Officer Harrison's gruff voice. "Please cooperate. Give the baby to Mr Peters and you can see him later."

"No."

"You really want to play it like this? We can do it the easy way or the hard way but it *is* going to happen, Saraya."

She opened her eyes and looked up at him in defiance. She hated him, every little thing about him. Flynn cried louder, fat tears rolling down his blotchy cheeks. She wiped them away with a finger tip and kissed his eyelids one at a time, her lips lingering on his satiny skin.

"I love you," she choked out, the lump in her throat strangling her words. "I love you so much." He gripped hold of her repeating her name with keening despair. "Mama, Mama, Mama." Her arms wrapped tighter around him, determined not to let him go.

Mr Peters held out his arms expectantly. "What is his name?"

"His name is Flynn," she answered automatically, the word like silk on her tongue. Still she could not bring herself to hand him over to the stranger, he would take him and she would never see him again. She *knew* it. But she didn't know what to do.

Her eyes darted around the room in panic, hoping for a miracle, an answer that would save her and Flynn, take them far away from this horrific place and let this all be just a bad dream. But there was nothing. Her arms were locked protectively around him, a cage to keep him safe from these predators.

"It's time now, Saraya."

She shook her head and a sob ripped through her. "I can't. You can't take him from me, it's not fair on him. He doesn't know you, he'll be terrified."

"He'll be fine. And it's only for a little while."

Saraya looked closely at Mr Peters. There was a special kind of evil in a man who could sound so sincere whilst trying to trick a woman into handing over her child. She knew he was lying. He made her skin crawl with hatred. She shook her head and looked down.

Mr Peters glanced at the two other men and gave a slight incline of his head. "Then I'm afraid we'll have to help you."

"No," she cried in panic. "Please, no, don't!" The two policemen leaned down, taking her arms firmly in their hands. "No! Stop!" she screamed in terror. "Please stop!"

Slowly, they prised open her arms and Mr Peters bent forward, scooping up the crying baby. He turned without a backwards glance and walked from the room with him. "Flynn!" she screamed. "Please, no! Bring him back, bring him back!" She struggled against their weight, trying to stand, to follow him, but they held her down until she knew it was too late. He was gone.

An animal moan emerged from the pit of her stomach and they finally released her arms. She collapsed on the floor in a heap, desperate cries racking her body, her face pushed into the soft woollen blanket which still held the sweet smell of her child.

Chapter Nineteen

Saraya often wondered if her parents, both biological and adoptive, had some vital part of them missing. From what she'd seen from the rest of the world, it seemed that the instinct to mother was embedded deep within the majority of women. For some it arrived early, for others, it took more time. But for most, it was there. Some felt it stronger, some resisted it and some could not control their urge to mother. It became who they were.

This was not just the case for humans, but for many other mammals too. A helpless infant strikes a passionate need within the female. She cannot help but care for it. The bonds of motherhood defy all reason. Yet, not one of her parents had ever put her first. They had been the exception to the rule, and Saraya had never dared to look closely at why that was.

She'd seen a documentary in her teens which had moved her deeply. It had been about inter-species adoption, so of course, she'd been fascinated. One story in particular had stuck in her mind. In Xinjiang, China, when a wolf cub was found starving and orphaned in the woods in 2005, a kindly farmer presented it to a nanny goat. Rather than attack the goat as its prey drive would command, the vulnerable cub sidled up to her and surprised everybody by suckling. His need for a mother overrode his instinct to hunt. And the goat, with all the love any mother can have for her child, accepted him unquestioningly, unconditionally, with no care for his differences.

The strength of love between a mother and child can erase every obstacle. Their need for each other comes before anything else. Her parents – all of them – may have been too broken to love her unconditionally, but Saraya knew that she hadn't inherited that trait. She could be the mother Flynn deserved. She would be the mother she wished she'd had for herself.

"So let me ask you again," Officer Harrison was saying. "What happened on the night of the twelfth?"

"I told you, I don't remember. I expect the usual, I

was at home feeding my son and putting him to bed. It's pretty much the same every night."

"And what if I told you I knew that child wasn't yours. That you had purposefully and knowingly taken him from his mother."

"No," Saraya said numbly. "I'd tell you that you were wrong. I'm his mother."

Officer Harrison cleared his throat and placed his hands heavily on the table, causing his coffee to spill over. He didn't seem to notice. "Miss Matthews, what is your relationship with this woman?" he asked, opening a file and pulling out a photograph of Emily. She was sporting a black eye and the picture was dated two years previously.

"I don't know her."

"Take a closer look." Saraya sighed and looked again. She could see Flynn when she looked at the curve of his mother's lips, the arch of her brows. Her heart jumped at the thought of him and she wondered if he was okay without her. PC Collins cleared his throat pointedly.

"I don't know her."

Officer Harrison sighed. "Tell me about the baby – Flynn," he asked. "Where was he born?"

"I had him at home. Unassisted."

"Convenient," he muttered.

"I preferred it that way. It felt safer without a bunch of strangers interfering," she said, meeting his eyes defiantly.

"Indeed. I assume you have proof of this."

Saraya shook her head. The only documents she would have for Flynn were the false ones she had asked Natalia to get, the ones that hadn't come in time to save them.

"No, not of the birth. I never registered him. I don't like the whole big brother thing. I wanted him to choose for himself when he was older."

PC Collins leaned forward in his chair, his breath hitting her hard in the face. It stank of stale coffee and onions. "What if I told you I don't believe a word you're saying? That I think you walked into a crime scene, and found a baby. That you decided to take matters into your own hands and take him, despite the fact you knew you shouldn't?" Saraya turned her face away remaining silent.

Officer Harrison put a hand up, cutting his colleague off. "Saraya, we all panic sometimes. We make mistakes. If you tell us the truth then we can treat this as a major lapse in judgement, rather than a premeditated crime. But the more you lie to us, the deeper you sink. Get out now, while you still can."

Saraya leaned back in her chair and crossed her arms. She was terrified. Each second that ticked by was a second that she was apart from Flynn, another second where he was scared and confused and being passed between strangers. She needed to get out of there. It occurred to her that any sensible person would have refused to talk without a lawyer present. But what was the point in a lawyer now? She was guilty. She'd taken him, and if they didn't already know that for sure, a simple DNA test would be all the proof they needed to end their investigation. She couldn't prove to them that she was innocent, because she wasn't.

She felt herself beginning to crumble, her muscles taught with the effort of holding herself together.

She couldn't speak for fear of falling apart. Could they not see how much she was suffering under their scrutiny? Could they not feel the desperation pulsing from her?

Officer Harrison stood and picked up a remote control. He pressed a few buttons and turned to Saraya, who avoided meeting his eyes. "Watch this." The screen flickered and then Saraya realised what she was seeing. The entrance to the bypass. Tim had been right, there was CCTV. *Shit.*

She watched, feigning nonchalance, though her palms began to itch and sweat. She could feel their eyes on her, burning into her mind as if they could pull out the answers they wanted. She saw Emily enter the bypass. She could tell by the skirt she wore and the way she moved, but the camera missed her face and the lump on her front could have simply been the cut of her coat rather than the baby Saraya knew she carried. The time in the left corner said 10.15p.m.

Officer Harrison skipped ahead to 11.45pm. Saraya swallowed and refused to avert her eyes, though she knew what was coming. She dug her nails into her palm as she watched the blurry image of a woman hesitating at the top of the stairs, before walking into the bypass. Again Saraya noticed thankfully that the camera had only caught the back of her head instead of her face.

The two police officers looked at her with expectant eyes, their brows raised in question. Saraya looked at them blankly. Officer Harrison shook his head. "Anything you want to say?" Saraya pursed her lips and shook her head. He grimaced, then switched the tape for a second one, and this time they were looking at the bypass from a different angle. The time read 11.57p.m. Saraya watched the darkness for a moment, and then a woman – her – ran out of the tunnel her arms wrapped tightly around a brown lumpy blanket. *Flynn!* she thought desperately. On the screen her face was lowered, her attention consumed with the bundle in her arms and once again, her identity was protected.

Saraya wanted to laugh with relief. *This* was their evidence? They had nothing. That could have been anyone. "Why are you showing me this?" she asked, her brow crossing in false confusion.

"We thought it might trigger some memories for you," PC Collins said, his tone verging on sarcastic. Saraya shook her head, her expression blank. She wouldn't speak another word, she wouldn't give them anything. "You have nothing you want to say?" he asked. Saraya shook her head and looked down at her lap. Officer Harrison and PC Collins exchanged a long look.

"Well," said Officer Harrison, standing up. "If that's the case, please wait here." He strode out of the room, closely followed by a sneering PC Collins. Saraya heard the door lock behind her and let out a whoosh of air, putting her head in her hands. What was going to happen to her? She couldn't be locked up, she just couldn't! How could she get Flynn back from inside a police cell? Her hands shook as she held back the tears. The seconds ticked by, slowly and painfully as she awaited their return. After what seemed like hours, though it was probably closer to thirty minutes, she heard movement outside the door and then Officer Harrison strode back in, a grim look on his face.

"It seems we don't have enough evidence to charge you. Yet," he said, putting great emphasis on the last word. "But you are under suspicion for the crime of child abduction and we want to see you back here in three days. Until then, you will be granted pre-charge bail."

Saraya almost giggled, her nerves jangling with excitement at the unexpected turn of events, but she managed somehow to hold back her relief. Officer Harrison watched her closely, his eyes narrow. "You will need to relinquish your passport today, of course."

"Of course. I understand," she choked out.

"And we will require you to take a DNA test too. Just a simple cheek swab," he smiled, though his eyes remained hard. Saraya's heart dropped. "If it matches the baby's, he will be returned to you promptly. In the meantime, he'll remain in foster care. The results will be back within the week." Saraya avoided his eyes, nodding her head numbly.

"And Miss Matthews, a word of advice for you. The courts will be far more sympathetic to a person who comes forward and admits their crime, *before* we have to spend taxpayers' money trying to find the answers ourselves. Do yourself a favour and think about it." Saraya said nothing, her head down as she waited. Officer Harrison sighed. "Go on then. PC Luton will accompany you home and collect your passport." Saraya nodded. They could have it, Natalia was bringing her a brand new identity anyway. They could take Saraya Matthews' freedom, she didn't care anymore. All she cared about was getting her baby back in her arms.

Evening had set in as she arrived back to her empty home in the police car. PC Luton was far less abrasive than PC Collins had been. She told Saraya to go inside and bring out her passport while she waited in the car. Saraya walked slowly up the dark path, Flynn's empty car seat in one hand. She tried not to look at it, the colourful swinging monkey toy taunting her from the thick plastic handle. Flynn *loved* that toy.

Why hadn't they thought to give it to him for comfort? It was the least they could have done. But of course they hadn't bothered to consider such a detail. They were cruel. Thoughtless. It was like rubbing salt in the wound, letting her take back the useless, empty seat without the baby in it.

She unlocked her front door and pushed it, feeling the resistance as it bumped up against something hard. Placing the car seat beside the door, she reached down, picking up the parcel, a brown paper package with her name scrawled across it in Natalia's familiar handwriting. *Thank goodness.*

She peeked inside and saw her new passport and papers. Grinning, she placed it on the table and went to get her real passport from the safe in the kitchen. She stepped back into the cold night air and handed it through the window of the car. "Thanks. See you in a few days," PC Luton said sombrely. Saraya watched her drive into the night and headed indoors. The quiet was unbearable.

She picked up the package containing her new identity and headed to the bedroom, placing it on the bedside cabinet. Without drawing the curtains or bothering to undress, she crawled under the covers and held her pillow to her face. It smelled of Flynn. It felt surreal being in bed without him, wrong and empty.

She knew what Tim would say if he were here now. That she should tell the truth. That she should admit her mistake and walk away, leaving Flynn to social services and the people trained to look after him. And hey, look on the bright side, it would mean that she could have uninterrupted sleep and enjoy a life of no responsibilities once again. She could hear him now, preaching about rules, about what society expected of her.

But Saraya would never do it. It hadn't been a mistake. She wouldn't undo it if she could. A full night's sleep and freedom from responsibility were the last things on her mind right now. She wanted to hear her baby snuffling beside her, as he woke needing milk or comfort under the blanket of darkness. She wanted to pace the bedroom floor, rocking him gently back to sleep as the birds stirred outside her window. She wanted to have someone relying on her, someone to make her a better person, someone to show her how good it can feel to love unconditionally and to give selflessly. She wanted Flynn.

Chapter Twenty

Saraya sat bolt upright in bed, sweat dripping down her back and neck, her hair plastered in clumps to her forehead. "Flynn!" she gasped, listening hard. She had heard him crying for her, she knew she had. Her heart pounded against her chest as she waited in the darkness. *Nothing*. He wasn't there. Just a dream.

Her body crumpled as the sleepy haze slowly left her and she realised with a devastating blow that she was totally alone. That keening cry had haunted her, dragged her from her slumber and now Saraya couldn't help but think about where her baby boy was. Who was soothing him as he searched fruitlessly for a familiar face? Was he being held and loved or was he shut away in a cold dark room, needing her as much as she needed him.

Anger coursed through her in overwhelming waves, fire spreading out through her limbs until her fingers and toes tingled with an urge to move. She wanted to hit something, to destroy every single thing that stood between her and her baby. How dare they take him without a care for what it would do to him? He'd already lost one mother and now he had lost another in less than a month. Handed over to strangers who didn't love him as she did, who wouldn't understand him as she could. She hated it, hated the people who had done this to them.

Her stomach clenched, nausea sweeping over her as she pounded her fist against her pillow in frustration. Was he *really* crying for her in that very moment? Had she sensed it deep within her? She had read about such connections between twins, or parents and children. Perhaps he really was desperately calling for her, yet she couldn't come.

She shuddered at the thought and squeezed her eyes tightly shut, her palms pushed deep into the sockets as she tried to dismiss the image of Flynn, his face tear stained and confused, from her tortured mind. The hairs on her arms raised as her thoughts spun, desperately trying to come up with a way to get him back. She didn't know what to do.

Being a mother was harder than she had ever imagined it could be. She no longer had the luxury of controlling her emotions, boxing her feelings up into carefully planned compartments. She couldn't console herself with a bowl of ice-cream and a long hot bath. The way she felt right now was nothing like a break up with a boyfriend, or losing a dear friend. The intensity of her feelings was unbearable, the aching loss of her child filled every inch of her being with desperate longing, tearing her apart from the inside out.

Saraya contemplated the words Tim had spoken to her during their last conversation. *"He's not really yours though, is he?"* But he was. She hadn't conceived him. She hadn't watched the swell of her belly bloom over the months as he grew within her womb. She hadn't felt the power of him moving through her body and out into the world as she birthed him, and she certainly hadn't planned for any of this. But none of that seemed to matter.

Being a mother, Saraya realised, was not just about creating a child. It was a feeling. A thousand strands of intricate silky web tying one person to another in an unbreakable and unconditional bond. She knew that even if she never set eyes on her son again, her feelings for him would remain, unwavering in their strength, for the rest of her life. Once you become a mother, you will always have the heart of a mother, one piece cut away and given as a gift to your child. And no matter what happens you can never get that piece back.

Failing to think of a solution, Saraya threw back the duvet and padded softly into the kitchen. The moon was full and bright, illuminating the room with a gentle glow. She ignored the light switch and instead made for the fridge where she found a nearly full bottle of Sauvignon blanc. She poured a glass and drank deeply, the burn of alcohol flowing warmly through her veins, comforting somehow.

A tear rolled slowly down her cheek as she stared blankly out of the window, her eyes trained on the perfectly round butterscotch moon. Her skin felt like it was crawling, the need to have her baby in her arms more powerful than any desire she had ever known. She knew that without him she would feel a cavernous loss for every moment of every day until she got him back.

She *wouldn't* give up. With a fire igniting in her blood, she suddenly realised that she would not stop. Flynn was hers, he belonged with her, needed her and there was nothing she wouldn't do to get him back. Nothing. As she poured another glass of wine, a calmness settled over her. For the first time since they prised him from her arms, she felt a certainty deep within her heart that this wasn't over. She wouldn't lose her baby. Flynn would be hers again.

She drank. The cool wine was beginning to make her head feel fuzzy, her heartbeat slowed to a more reasonable pace and she smiled, suddenly noticing the cabbage patch Flynn she had bought that very first outing, strewn across a cushion on the rocking chair.

In two short strides she reached him, placing her wine on the floor and gently scooping him into her arms as if he were a real baby. She cradled him gently to her chest and began to hum a lullaby, the same one she had sung every single night to Flynn as he had fallen asleep in her arms, his breath falling sweetly on her chest as she stroked his hair and kissed his cheeks.

She swayed in the darkness, singing and clutching her hands tightly around the soft body of the doll, turning in circles as she murmured the haunting words. Her back hit the cool edge of the fridge and her song ceased as she felt her body lose the will to continue. Her legs gave out from under her as she slid heavily to the floor. A sob broke free and then she was struggling to catch her breath, the tears falling fast as she choked on the bitter taste of despair. She balled herself into a tight coil, her arms never releasing the doll as her cheek hit the cold hard tile. Her sobs racked her body until she could cry no more.

Chapter Twenty-One

There was a banging coming from somewhere far off. It echoed through Saraya's brain, sleep still fogging her thoughts. She remained unmoving, wishing the agonising noise would cease. Instead, it grew stronger, every whack reverberating through her bones. Saraya tried and failed to open an eye. The sticky lid was glued shut, swollen and tender from too many tears. Her head throbbed and beneath her she could feel a cold, hard surface. A shiver worked its way through her body.

Lifting a heavy arm up to her face, she dragged a hand over her eyes clearing the crusted sleepy dust away. With difficulty she slowly willed her eyelids to open, the harsh light causing her to squint and groan. The relentless banging continued and now she could hear someone calling her name too. It seemed far off and distant to her clouded, confused mind.

Saraya was only half surprised to find herself lying horizontally on her kitchen floor. Cabbage patch Flynn was cuddled close to her chest and as the world came into focus she saw the empty wine bottle on its side, rolled halfway across the tile.

She groaned again and placed a cool palm on her aching head. "Where is he?" she whispered desperately, Flynn already consuming her thoughts entirely, the sick feeling in the pit of her stomach having nothing to do with her hangover.

The banging reached a new level of intensity and now Saraya recognised the voice calling her name. *Tim.* She slowly pulled herself up to standing and braced herself against the fridge, overcome with a dizzying head rush. On wobbly legs, she made her way to the front door and opened it slowly. Tim looked as frazzled as she felt. He pushed his way past her and into the hallway, spinning to look at her in all her dishevelled glory.

"Close the door," he commanded. Saraya swung it shut and stared at him. "God, Saraya, I heard what happened. *Fuck.* Are you okay?" he asked, stepping forward to place his hands on her shoulders.

"Okay?" she tasted the word on her tongue. It was sour. "They have taken my child. How could I possibly be okay?" she spat. "But don't worry, I didn't mention your name. You're not going to get dragged in as an accomplice."

"Oh, Saraya," he shook his head. "I'm here because I'm worried about you, not because I'm scared for myself, you idiot." He wrapped his arms around her. She was stiff under his touch, fighting back the tears that threatened to fall again.

"They took him right out of my arms, Tim," she whispered. "He was so scared, so very scared and I couldn't stop them. I can't bear it, I don't know what to do."

Tim sighed and stroked her hair. "I know. I'm so sorry." He leaned back. "Look, I know this is the last thing you want to hear, but I'm going to say it anyway. Maybe this was for the best, you know, that it happened before he got too comfortable with you? I mean, this way he still has time to start again with another family. He'll forget all of this and you can both move on."

"Move on?" her tone was cold and dangerous as she pushed away from his arms. "Move on? They have taken my child. How on earth am I supposed to move on? That baby needs to be with me. I am the only mother he's got. Why in the world would you think telling me he'll forget me would make things better? He may not know why, but this will cause a sadness inside him that he'll carry for his whole life. He's already carrying the burden of Emily's death and now you want me to be happy that he's got more scars on his heart?"

"I'm sorry. It's raw, I know." He bowed his head sadly. "I should leave."

"Why did you even come, Tim?" she asked angrily. "Certainly not to help me feel better." She walked away from him, heading for the living room, but suddenly spun back towards him. "Wait a minute, how did you know he was gone?" she asked, her voice filled with urgency. "How come you're here? Are you working on his case? Tim, are you?"

"No, I'm not, but it's all everyone was talking about in the office this morning. I came as soon as I heard what happened."

Saraya sucked in a breath. "Tim, do you know

where he is?" she asked, her fingernails cutting tracks into her already shredded palms. He shook his head wordlessly. A lump filled her throat as she grasped onto a tiny flicker of hope. "Tim, answer me. Where have they taken him? Where's my baby?"

"He's not yours, Saraya. He never will be. I can't help you," he answered sadly.

"You can and you have to!" she cried. "This isn't right, Tim and you fucking know it. He needs me! As far as he's concerned *I'm* his mother now that Emily isn't here, and now he's lost me – the one person he can count on. This is the second time he has had to be pulled from the arms of the person he most needs. It's unthinkable, Tim, how can you put him through this?" She dropped her head into her hands in anguish. "And I'm going to go to prison. For something as simple as loving a baby who needed me. I'll never see him again," she shook her head, her voice cracking with the power of her emotions.

"Tim, this is wrong, you know it. Open your mind and see past the law – what does your heart tell you?" He turned his back on her, bracing his hands against the front door, his forehead creased with conflict. "Tim!" she pushed.

"I think..." he sighed, turning back to her. "Actually, I know. I know you would be a wonderful mother to him. You are loving and patient and funny, and he would be lucky to have you. But it's too late for that now. Maybe if you'd done the right thing when you found him, you could have been in his life somehow. Maybe. But what can you do now? It's all out in the open and you'll never be allowed near him, Saraya. I'm sorry."

"But I could be, Tim. If I could get him back, I could keep him safe. I just need you to tell me where he is."

"And then what? Bring him back here and wait for the Old Bill to come knocking?"

"No."

"This isn't a game, Saraya, you can't play hide and seek with the law. You'll be caught and you'll never get bail after that. And you can forget getting a lenient sentence if you steal him from under his foster carers nose, it won't happen. They'll throw you in a cell for years."

Saraya took a chance and decided to tell him everything. She had nothing left to lose. "I can leave. Today. I have money, false passports, it's all ready to go. I just need Flynn. I'll leave and we won't ever come back."

Tim sucked in a breath and stared at her. "Are you serious?" She nodded. "You would really do that? Leave your home, your country, everything you know, just so you can have him?"

"I would do *anything*."

"You really would, wouldn't you?" he gave a half smile. "You aren't who I thought you were, Saraya. You are so much stronger than I ever realised. It might not be the best time to say it, but I'm proud of you. I wonder what we could have been to each other if we had let down our guard and been open. Shown each other our true hearts." She dipped her chin, nodding slowly, his words making her feel nothing but sadness. "But," he continued, "I guess we'll never know." He reached into his pocket and drew out a folded piece of paper. Saraya watched him with hawklike eyes.

"I must be crazy. I'll lose everything if this gets out, you understand?" He held the paper tantalisingly between his fingers. "But I do this job because I want to help children have a better life, and strange as it may seem, I know that's exactly what this baby will have with you," he smiled. "But please, let this be the last thing you ask of me. I won't help you again." He stepped forward and pushed the paper into her palm. She grasped it reverently, feeling as though he had just handed her a winning lottery ticket.

"Thank you," she choked out, tears streaming unashamedly down her cheeks. "Thank you so much."

"Where will you go?"

"I don't know. Far. They won't find us."

"Be safe. Be careful."

"I will," she swallowed.

He kissed her softly on the mouth and pulled back to look her in the eye. "Goodbye, Saraya Matthews. Have a good life." He touched a thumb to her swollen lips and smiled.

"I won't make you regret this, Tim. I swear." She watched him open the door, walk through it and throw her a final parting glance, before pulling it closed behind him. She stared silently at it for a moment. Then she wiped the back of her hand over her cheeks, drying her tears. The time for crying was over. Her baby was waiting for her.

Chapter Twenty-Two

The waistband of the grey trouser suit was rubbing irritatingly against her hip. She wriggled in the driver's seat of her parked Fiat, running her fingers along the rough seam. It had been so long since she had worn anything resembling office attire and she realised she hadn't missed it in the slightest. Her clothes of late had been tailored to her new lifestyle. She wanted comfy jeans and floaty skirts, things that she could throw on in a hurry and roll around on the carpet in. But she needed to dress the part for what she was about to do.

She watched the house across the road in nervous anticipation. She had wasted no time after Tim had left. Her suitcase was packed to the brim with her things and Flynn's, and stored safely in the boot of her car. The fake passports were tucked carefully into her handbag, along with a wedge of twenties, and she had made some calls to check that her new bank account was up and running.

Natalia had taken her life savings and worked her

magic on the money, moving it around through various channels until there was no trace of Saraya Matthews left on it. It was ready and waiting for her under the new name of Miss Amelia Foster in her brand new account. She was as prepared as she could be, and nothing was going to stand in her way.

Except for the foster carer who had her baby. Saraya had already knocked once, but there was nobody home. And now she had been waiting for two hours in her freezing car. She hoped she wasn't being watched by the neighbours, but she was too scared that she would miss them coming home if she circled the block, so she stayed put and tried to look inconspicuous.

The thought of seeing Flynn again made her giddy with joy. She had packed his favourite toys and snacks in the changing bag and had the sling ready under the seat. Her hands shook with impatience as she waited for a glimpse of him.

The sound of a baby crying roused her from her slump at once and her eyes shot to the racket. A tired looking woman with shoulder length blonde hair was pushing a buggy, three other children trailing along behind her. Saraya's eyes honed in on the pushchair. She could just make out a dark tuft of hair, but that was enough. She would know that cry anywhere – it was Flynn!

It took every ounce of her strength not to rush out of the car and scoop him up into her arms. His cry was painful to hear and the blank, haggard face of the woman pushing him, led her to believe he had cried so long she had given up trying to soothe him. Saraya swallowed back tears and bit her lip hard in an effort not to call out his name.

"Mummy!" shouted one of the children, a girl of around three. She walked beside a boy who had such similar features to her, Saraya was certain they were twins. "Mummy, I want a drink!"

"We're nearly home, you can have one in a minute," the woman replied, a shimmer of stress permeating her voice.

"I want one now!" The little girl stopped walking and sat on the pavement, her arms folded crossly over her knees.

"Molly, I am going to make you some lunch and a drink as soon as we get inside. Now stand up," her mother demanded.

"No!" she replied crossly, turning her face away and jutting out her chin. A third child, a boy of around seven was dawdling behind, running a stick along the garden walls as he passed them. He was obviously lost in a world of his own and not paying any attention to where he was going. As she watched Saraya could see a branch on the verge ahead of him.

"Hurry up please, Adam, we need to get on," the woman called in his direction.

"Okay, Mummy," he said, his eyes still fixed on the wall. He sped up and a moment later, collided with the branch, tripping over and landing in a heap on the ground. As he lifted his head, Saraya saw an angry graze on his cheekbone. The boy sat up, rubbing his elbow, his face twisted in discomfort. For a tense second he was silent and then, as if someone flicked a switch, an almighty bellow erupted from him.

His mother looked up from trying to cajole the

little girl off the ground and turned towards him. "Oh for goodness sake, Adam! What are you doing down there? Get up and stop being so silly!"

"I can't," he cried. "I've hurt my arm and my face is bleeding. Look!"

"Oh god." She took a deep breath and rubbed her eyes. Flynn was still screaming, his voice hoarse now. Saraya couldn't stand the sound, but she forced herself to stay put.

"Right! We need to get home, now. Molly! Get up or get left behind. Adam, if your arm is hurt, there is no reason you can't use your legs. Now, let's get indoors and we can have a good look at you and clean you up. And yes, I will get you a bloody drink, Molly. Come on!" She turned without a backwards glance and pushed the buggy up the driveway, leaving the three children behind. The little boy followed, and realising she was serious, Molly and Adam picked themselves up and ran to catch up too. They went through the door and it slammed shut behind them.

Saraya took a deep steadying breath, counted to five and stepped out of the car. She felt utterly wretched at what she was about to do, but that wasn't enough to stop her. She walked up the driveway, straightened her navy blue blouse and rapped sharply on the door. She could hear a rumble of shouting voices coming from inside, more crying still, and she pulled herself up into a rigid statue, holding her wild emotions tightly inside.

The door flew open and the woman stood before her with blood streaked across the back of her hand, her eyes narrowed. "Yes?" she asked curtly.

Saraya stepped forward. "Mrs Walker?"

"Yes?"

"I'm Laura Wilkins, from social services," she said briskly, flashing an identification badge at her. "I presume my colleague called you this morning to let you know I was coming?"

The woman shook her head, flustered. "Oh, no, I'm sorry I didn't get a call." She reached into her back pocket and pulled out her phone. "Oh, it's off! I'm so sorry, I always forget to charge it. What did you need to know?"

"That's quite alright," Saraya said with a warm

smile. "I've come to collect the baby in your care." She reached into her bag and pulled out a typed piece of paper. "Ah, yes, Flynn. Is that him I hear crying?" she asked, trying to keep her voice steady.

"Uh, yes, it is I'm afraid. He's been rather unsettled since he arrived. Nothing seems to soothe him."

Saraya swallowed and nodded. "I see."

"We were expecting him to be here for a while though," Mrs Walker said.

"I know. Circumstances have changed though, so if you could gather his things together and say your goodbyes, I'll take him with me now."

"Now?"

"Yes, Mrs Walker. Unless there's a reason he can't come?"

"Mummy!" came an angry scream from the back of the house. "I told you I'm thirsty!"

"Just a minute, Molly!"

Adam walked through to the hall, his face smeared with scarlet streaks. "Look, Mummy, it's bleeding again."

"Oh, for goodness sake! Where's the cloth I gave

you?"

"I put it in the wash."

"Well get another out of the drawer please and hold it there until I come in. I won't be long."

Saraya took a step forward. "I can see you've got your hands full."

"Yes, I'm so sorry. Just a second and I'll grab Flynn and his bag. I haven't had a chance to unpack it yet what with this lot keeping me in check."

"Of course. I'll wait here." She rushed up the stairs and Saraya heard a door bang open. A few second later, Mrs Walker ran back down again with a bag under her arm. "There's his stuff and I'll just get him out of the buggy."

Saraya nodded, tight lipped, unable to speak a word. Mrs Walker disappeared behind a door and Saraya looked back over her shoulder, assessing the deserted street, her stomach clenched into a tight ball of anticipation. Her breathing was ragged as she listened to Flynn's angry screams growing louder still as Mrs Walker picked him up. Finally, she emerged through the doorway trying to hold a squirming, thrashing Flynn. Saraya's heart skipped a beat as her eyes fell on him.

"Good luck," Mrs Walker said, handing him to her. "He's quite a handful.

Saraya took him against her, resisting the threatening tears as she felt his weight in her arms at last. He screamed and kicked against her. "It's okay, sweetie, it's okay," Saraya said softly, holding back all the words she needed to say but couldn't in the presence of his foster mother.

Flynn's eyes flew wide open and his cries ceased immediately. He fixed her with a desperate stare, his body quivering as he reached out a hand and grasped hold of her cheek. His sharp little fingernails sunk into her skin, but she didn't move a muscle. His head sank into her chest as he curled himself into the foetal position and tried to get as close to her as he possibly could. She wrapped her arms tightly around him and kissed his downy head.

"Wow," Mrs Walker exclaimed. "You must have the magic touch!"

"So I'm told," Saraya replied, forcing a smile. "I

think he's just tired. He'll probably start screaming the moment I put him in the car seat," she joked stiffly.

"Well, I'll leave you to attend to your other little ones then," Saraya said, nodding towards the little girl who had just stepped out of the kitchen covered in what looked suspiciously like chocolate milk.

"Oh, Molly! Look at the state of you," Mrs Walker exclaimed. "Yes, thank you and goodbye Flynn." She patted him on the cheek gently and Flynn turned away from her, burrowing his face into Saraya's shirt.

"We'll be in touch," Saraya smiled. She turned towards the road and heard the door shut behind her as the busy woman went to help her other children. Saraya walked in a direct line to her car, revelling in the feeling of rightness that had settled over her the moment she had held Flynn in her arms once again. She moved his car seat from the back into the passenger seat. She needed to be able to see him and hold his hand, and she knew he needed it too.

She threw his bag in the back of the car before tucking him safely into the little pod. Climbing into the driver's seat, she bent down to kiss him gently on his red, tear stained cheeks. He sighed and watched her with sleepy, bloodshot eyes. "Oh my darling, I'm so sorry I wasn't there when you needed me, I'm so sorry. But I swear on my life, I will never let that happen to us again." She forced herself to sit up, her back poker straight as she held herself together.

Her job was only half done, and the hardest step was yet to come. They would have time to cry together later, and she would hold him close and try to help him heal from this trauma, but for now, they had to get going. She turned the key in the ignition and drove away from the scene of yet another crime, one hand cradled around her sweet son's face as he drifted off to sleep at last.

Chapter Twenty-Three

It felt like they had been on the road for hours, every minute stretching on an age, each mile tortuously long. Saraya's nerves were frayed as she glanced in her rear view mirror every few seconds, expecting to see blue flashing lights approaching at speed. At last, with a sense of exhausted relief, she saw the rusty yellow sign for the place she was looking for and swung her car left, driving under the barrier and into the car park behind the little run down looking café.

She knew she was putting a lot of faith in Natalia at this point of her journey, but she needed her help. For the second time in as many weeks, she found herself with no choice but to put her trust in her old, wayward friend. She could only hope that she wouldn't let her down.

Only one other car was parked in the car park, a fairly inconspicuous silver Corsa, long overdue a trip to the carwash. It didn't look like the sort of car Nat would choose, but Saraya presumed that was entirely the point. She wouldn't want to be caught up in suspicion, linked to her and Flynn in any way.

Saraya leaned over from her seat and unstrapped Flynn, bringing him to her lap. He was still very sleepy as he leaned his head heavily against her chest, a gurgle of relief escaping his soft pink lips. Saraya held back tears as she thought of him screaming for her, exhausted yet unable to sleep or rest, surrounded by strangers in an unfamiliar home. Thank goodness she had found a way to get him back.

A wave of guilt washed over her as she thought of Mrs Walker. That poor woman would be in a world of trouble when it was discovered that she had given the baby in her care, to a strange woman at the door. Saraya had been surprised at just how easy it had been to con her into giving him up. She doubted Mrs Walker would ever be able to foster again. But then, if she was going to go around handing out babies to the first person who knocked at the door, perhaps that was a good thing, she reasoned.

Saraya felt anger bloom as she pictured her now. Why was she fostering in the first place? Was she doing it for the money? She clearly had too much on her plate already, without taking on a baby who needed so much love and attention to heal his past. He needed to be held. *Comforted.* Poor little Flynn had been screaming in that buggy for going on twenty minutes, and who knows how long before that. She couldn't care for him properly, and she shouldn't have taken him if that was the case.

Saraya sighed, feeling angry with herself now. She didn't want to hurt anyone, she didn't want to bring stress and trouble to that woman and her family. All she wanted was to have her son back, to give him the love he deserved and save him from a life of being shepherded from home to home, never knowing the strength of a mother's love. She was sorry Mrs Walker had been caught up in it, but she wasn't sorry she had taken him. She would do it again in an instant.

She sighed again, breathing deeply as she inhaled the scent of Flynn's head. He smelled different, like strong washing powder and air freshener. Saraya wanted to bath him and clear away all traces of the whole ordeal. To wash the last few days away and find herself snuggled in bed with her son moulded safely against her. But their journey was not yet over.

She steeled herself, and stepped from the car, settling Flynn on her hip as she made her way to the front of the café. The wooden door frame was visible beneath the peeling yellow paint. *Nicotine yellow,* Saraya thought as she tried the handle. It didn't budge. The place looked closed, and Saraya peered through the frosted glass. No light or movement came from within.

Her nerves building, Saraya rapped smartly three times on the door. She waited. Nothing. She put her hands up to the glass and tried to see inside. She couldn't make out a thing. She knocked once more, unsure what she should do, and then at last, she heard movement from within.

"Who's there?" a male voice demanded.

"Um, I'm supposed to be meeting a friend here."

"Who?"

"Uh... Nat – Natalia."

The metal handle jerked downwards and the door swung open. There stood a lanky, blonde haired man in his early twenties, and beside him a beaming Natalia.

"Babe! You fucking did it! I knew you would. Quick, come inside, come inside." Saraya found herself pulled into the darkness of the building and heard the door slam shut behind them. The blonde man was locking it again. Saraya's eyes slowly adjusted to the dim light as she looked round the room. There were dusty tables dotted here and there, chairs stacked haphazardly on top of them. Flynn was looking around alertly now too, his fingernails bedding deep down into Saraya's shoulder, waves of fear streaming from him. Saraya felt her heart jolt in sympathy for him. Of course the poor baby was scared. She didn't attempt to remove his nails from her skin.

"Hello, sweetheart," Natalia crooned uncharacteristically at the baby, tickling his cheek with a long blue fingernail. "It's good to see you again."

Saraya stared at her in surprise. "Are you quite alright, Nat? You're going all soft!" she laughed. "I don't think I have ever seen you talk to a baby like that before."

"Well, this one's special, isn't he?" She blew Flynn a kiss and he gave her a shy smile, bobbing his head into the safety of Saraya's shoulder as he watched Natalia curiously.

"Well, don't expect you wanna be hanging around too long," the man piped up. "Let's get started, shall we?"

"Yep. Saraya, this is Bill, he's going to take your car to the scrap yard now and get that gone for you. You can get the bus to the airport, it goes from just round the corner. Bill, go and get her bags and bring them here," Natalia instructed him.

"Oh, Flynn's sling, it's under the passenger seat, can you get that too, please?" Saraya asked as she handed him the keys. He nodded and made for the door, unlocking it and locking it behind him as he went.

"He's thorough," Saraya remarked with a raised eyebrow.

"Better than the alternative," she smiled back. "Right, come on." She walked towards the back of the wide, dusty room and opened the door behind the counter. "The kitchen has no windows so no prying eyes to peek in on us," she said. "Follow me."

Saraya followed her through the café and into the kitchen. Natalia shut the door behind them. It was light in here, the long strip lighting blaring brightly, illuminating the cold silver tops of the stainless steel workbenches. "Right, now sit down here and I'll sort your hair and make-up," Natalia told her firmly, pointing to a wooden chair she'd obviously brought in from the front earlier. "Quickly, we don't have much time to transform you into, who was it?" she pondered, picking up a pair of sharp silver scissors. "Ah, Amelia Foster, that's it. I like it,"

"Thanks," Saraya said, taking a seat and letting Natalia go at her hair with wild abandon. "It'll take some getting used to I think."

"You'd be surprised. I think you're ready to forget Saraya Matthews and move on to something better," Natalia said, leaning over her shoulder to look her in the eye. "And what could be better than getting to be this little one's mummy?"

"I really can't believe *you're* saying these words,"

Saraya laughed. "Anyone would think you're getting broody."

"Well, maybe I am."

"Really?"

"Yes, really. Watching you and little Flynny at dinner the other night, I don't know, it did something to me. I felt something, jealousy I think, watching the connection you two have. It's special, Saraya. I want that too."

"Wow. That's great, Nat. It's bloody hard work though."

"I know. But it must be worth it. I mean, look at you, look at what you're willing to do for him."

Saraya smiled at her. "Yes, it's worth it. *He's* worth it." She sat back and stroked her fingers through his hair, listening to him babbling away to himself, while Natalia worked on her.

"You've saved him from a life of feeling unwanted, you know," she said quietly. "He'll thank you one day." Saraya shook her head, swallowing thickly as a lump filled her throat. Natalia stopped cutting and began smoothing a strong smelling crème through her locks.

"Dye?" Saraya asked.

"Yep. Your hair is so dark it won't be a dramatic change, but it should be lighter by a few shades if we leave it on for the full time. I'll do your face while we wait." She washed her hands and moved to sit in front of Saraya, winking at Flynn as she rifled through her make up bag. He squealed loudly and tried to grab for the mascara, but Natalia handed him an eyelash comb instead and he leaned back against Saraya, investigating it with the utmost concentration. Natalia worked quickly, the tip of her tongue poking out ever so slightly as she appraised her canvas.

After a while, she put her make-up kit to one side and took Flynn from Saraya's lap, placing him on her coat on the floor. She led Saraya over to a sink, pouring shampoo into her hand and lathering it in, rinsing the dye from her hair. After she wrapped a towel around her head, she pulled out a pair of jeans and a cream cowl neck jumper from her bag. "Right, strip off and let's get you in these clothes. You won't be needing that suit where you're going," she smiled. Saraya shuffled out of the stuffy business outfit with relief, pulling on the comfortable jeans and jumper instead. Natalia handed her a pair of green corduroy dungarees and a white long sleeve vest for Flynn.

"You'd better change him too," she said. "We want him as unrecognisable as possible. I'm not going to dye his hair though, we'll just pop a hat on him and hope he isn't spotted."

"I don't know how long it will take for them to realise he's gone," Saraya said, as she undressed the wriggling baby. "Could be hours, could be a day or two if we're lucky. I would have thought that social services would be checking up on him regularly, but who knows?"

"We can't know. But the sooner you're on a plane and out of here, the safer you'll be."

Saraya stood up and rubbed the towel through her hair. It felt soft and stopped even shorter than she was used to. She liked it already. Natalia gave her a quick blast of the hair-dryer and then held up a mirror for her to see. She looked different, definitely different. More free. The make-up had brightened her skin and lifted her eyes. Her lips were fuller, natural pink and glossy and her hair was a warm auburn shade. She looked like a version of herself she had strived to discover for years, and she realised with a smile that it had nothing to do with the makeover and everything to do with stripping away the layers of herself, to discover who she was deep within her heart.

"Thank you," she said to Natalia, her expression filled with emotion as their eyes met. "I don't know what I would have done without you to help me through this."

"You would have found a way. I know you would." Natalia picked up Flynn and kissed him on the cheek. He pushed away from her and reached his arms out to Saraya who scooped him up eagerly. They walked through the kitchen and back out to the café where Saraya's suitcase and Flynn's sling were stacked carefully by the door. There was no sign of Bill, but the key to the café was lying on the doormat.

"He will have locked us in to make sure we weren't interrupted," Natalia said. "You be okay from here?"

"We will." Saraya reached forward and hugged her

friend tightly. "Thank you. And just so you know, I think you'll be a fantastic mother." Natalia pecked her on the cheek and blew a kiss for Flynn. Saraya buckled up the sling and fastened it around him, reaching for the handle of her suitcase. Natalia unlocked the door and it swung open.

"Don't stop for anything, don't waste time and don't look back," she instructed.

"I won't."

"And Saraya," she called, as she walked out into the cold. "Don't lose him again."

Chapter Twenty-Four

The airport was packed. Saraya made her way through the overheated departures hall, her bulging suitcase balancing precariously on a trolley. She hadn't eaten a morsel all day long and her stomach churned with the acidic remains of last nights liquid over indulgence. She couldn't get over the feel of Flynn's soft little body against hers, the angel tuft of fluffy dark hair, the heady scent of his baby breath. She was in heaven.

She pushed her way through the slew of tourists and travellers, making her way to the departures board. She'd spent her time in the car outside the foster home wisely this morning, checking online to see what was available, and now she had three possible options for outbound flights this afternoon. Looking at the blinking board she saw that the 3.45 p.m. flight to Goa was delayed by four hours.

That one's out the window then, she thought decisively. That left the 4 p.m. flight to Colombo, Sri Lanka, or the 4.15 p.m. flight to Cancún, Mexico. She patted her pockets for her phone to check the time, only to realise she no longer had it. She had left it in her car for Bill to dispose of. She couldn't risk being traced by it.

Instead, she lifted her wrist and gazed at the new watch adorning it. She'd have to get used to doing that until she could get a new phone. 2.20 p.m. already. She just about had time to get either one if she hurried, but there wasn't time for much deliberation. "Where do you fancy, Flynny?" she muttered under her breath. "Spicy food or cheesy food? Both have good beaches... But I don't have a clue what language they speak in Sri Lanka. Hmm..." she pondered, wondering if her GCSE Spanish would be enough to get by on. It would have to be. Besides, English was probably spoken by a big chunk of the population in a country so close to America, she reasoned.

"Mexico it is then," she said with a decisive smile. She saw the ticket desk across the hall and made her way over to it, standing in line behind a young family. The little boy, Saraya guessed to be around six years old, was on the floor racing a car around the base of the desk, whilst his parents collected their tickets. He looked up at her, smiling.

"That's a nice baby," he said. "Can I see him?" Saraya hesitated for a second, before leaning down gently to let the boy peer in at the sleeping baby cocooned in the sling. "He's nice. We're going on holiday, on an aeroplane!" he told her proudly. "I went on one before, but I was just a baby then and I don't remember it. So this might as well be my first time."

Saraya nodded and smiled. Out of the corner of her eye she could see two security guards watching her. No, not just watching her, *pointing* at her. She looked over her shoulder, hoping to see something there that had caught their attention. She was being paranoid, surely. But no, there was nothing there. The little boy continued to talk, his voice muffling in her ears as she broke out in a cold sweat. She tried to keep her eyes trained on the child, to look calm, innocent, though she felt like a wreck.

She cast a swift glance over to the guards once

again and sucked in a breath. They were walking towards her. There was no doubt in her mind, they were coming, right now. She chewed her bottom lip nervously and her arm tightened instinctively around Flynn. She had no choice but to front it out. She needed to get on a plane and fast, and it wasn't as if she could just turn and make a run for it. That would end everything for her and Flynn.

"Excuse me, Miss?"

Saraya looked up with mock surprise. "Yes?" she asked sweetly, forcing a warm smile. "Can I help you?" The two guards eyed each other as if waiting for the other to speak. Saraya waited in silence. The little boy pulled at her arm.

"We're going now!" he exclaimed, his voice brimming with excitement." His mum threw Saraya a weary smile and a roll of her eyes, a look of sheer camaraderie that made Saraya feel like she belonged. That she too was in the mothers' club, where they each instinctively knew what the other was going through. If it wasn't for the fact that she was still waiting for the two guards to rip her world apart, it would have felt wonderful. Finally one of the men cleared his throat.

"I'm sorry, I can see you're next in line so we won't keep you. Ben here, has just had a baby," the guard said, clapping his colleague on the shoulder.

"Well, my wife has," Ben laughed.

"And he's been complaining that his wife can't go out anywhere, coz' the little one screams bloody murder in the pram, see?"

"So," Ben interrupted again, "we were just admiring this carrier contraption thingy you've got here, and wondering where I could get one for our little one. It looks like it might be just the ticket."

Saraya burst into a wide smile, relief flooding through her like a river of warm honey. They wanted to know about the sling! She wasn't caught, it wasn't over.

She held her hand as steady as she could manage, as she wrote down the name of the baby carrier on a piece of paper she borrowed from the woman at the ticket desk. Then she watched in disbelief as they walked away with jovial smiles, leaving her to her freedom. She handed over her new credit card and bought the tickets in the names Amelia Foster and Rory Foster. Within minutes, she had checked in her one suitcase and they were heading through the departures gates.

Her heart was beating like a hummingbird's wings as she looked around at the vast number of security guards in this area. She breathed in and handed over the two passports and boarding passes to be checked.

"Fancy a bit of Winter sunshine, eh?" said the guard as he opened the passports, scrutinising the photographs. Saraya tried to answer but found her throat blocked by an enormous lump, her tongue plastered to the roof of her bone dry mouth. Instead she settled for nodding and smiling. Flynn began to stir and she was thankful for the distraction, busying herself with him. The passports were mercifully handed back to her, and she was on to the next hurdle.

She put her bag on the conveyor belt, and transferred Flynn's bottles into a clear bag, dropping them into a tray. She was just deliberating about whether or not she should take Flynn out of the sling, and put that on the belt too, when a security guard called to her.

"Hey, Miss!" Saraya looked up, feeling panicked. "Come here," the woman said, standing beside the metal detector. Saraya swallowed and walked over to her.

"Yes?"

"You don't need to take off the sling. Leave the baby in it and walk through here, please."

"Oh, okay... thanks." She walked through the security archway, only to jump when it emitted a loud beep.

"Have you removed your belt? Jewellery?" the guard asked. Saraya's hand went to the watch at her wrist.

"No, sorry," she said unclasping it and handing it over. "Here." She was made to walk through again, and this time there was no alarm. In disbelief, she collected her things and walked away, heading for her gate.

She couldn't believe it. The passports were

excellent, she knew. When she saw them for the first time she had been amazed at how good they were. But she had still wondered if they would be good enough. Would the airport security see them right away for the fakes they really were? Would they have ways of checking, that Natalia's contacts hadn't predicted? So far she had been lucky, beyond lucky. But she wasn't there yet.

She checked the time again. 3.40 p.m. The board hanging at gate number seven said her flight would open for boarding at 3.45 p.m. *Good timing,* she thought. She paced nervously for a minute, looking out of the wide window at the plane which would take her away. Suddenly, realising her pacing might make her look suspicious, she stopped. She briefly looked around, and then headed towards a vending machine, where she scrambled with a handful of coins to buy a bottle of water. She then made her way over to a hard plastic seat by the window and forced herself to sit down.

This was it then. She was leaving England and she had no idea if she would ever be able to return. The reality began to seep in. Up until now she had been consumed with one thing and one thing only. Flynn's safety. Getting him away from the people who would take him without a thought for his emotional needs, who would thrust him into uncertainty and a life of being passed around like a puppet, all for the misguided belief that it was for his own good. She had been so focused on what she was gaining in becoming his mother, she hadn't spared a thought for what she was giving up.

Before Flynn, she hadn't had much of a life, it was true. But it had been safe and familiar. She had known that when she set out for her Sunday morning jog, she would pass through the same green parks. She would see the trees which had been growing for hundreds of years, pass the same buildings and landmarks. She knew that her family were just a train ride away, and her predictable, kind and occasionally funny boyfriend was there when she needed comfort or distraction.

Now, she was heading into something new. Something unknown and scary, and for the first time in her life she was doing it alone, without anyone to lean on. It was mad and frightening, but it was also real. She had craved something true, something deep to connect to and throw herself into for as long as she could remember.

She didn't want life to be a safe little bubble, unchanging and unchallenging. *That* life held no appeal for her now. She was ready to head into the world with a new name, a new purpose, needing nothing more than the love of her child to give her courage. She was ready.

Static crackled over the Tannoy, and then an announcement was being made. Boarding for flight VS93 to Cancún was now open. Families with small children and first class were welcome to board. This was it.

Saraya made her way over to the forming queue and waited her turn to hand over her boarding passes and passports to one of the smiling staff. She held her breath, and a moment later was being wished a lovely flight and shepherded into the claustrophobic gloom of the tunnel leading down to the aeroplane.

She was directed to her seat, and a kind flight attendant brought her a lap belt for Flynn who would be riding with her, and told her to call if she needed anything else. "I know it's not easy travelling alone with a little baby," he smiled warmly, patting Flynn gently on the head.

"Thank you," she nodded as he walked away, surprised to find herself blinking back hot tears. The tension flowing through her was almost unbearable. She was so close, but it wasn't enough just yet. Flynn smacked his chubby hands against the window, as Saraya flicked her eyes between the outside and the aisle of the plane. Every time she saw an official looking person, she stopped breathing. Her hands shook and she felt faint, but she couldn't let it show.

When a man took the empty seat beside her she nearly jumped out of her skin, but managed to just about hold herself together and offer him an apologetic smile. "If it makes you feel better, I think he'll sleep a good chunk of the way," she told him, looking at Flynn with love in her eyes.

"No worries. I'm used to kids, my sister has five

and I love them all. Don't stress about it," he smiled. Saraya nodded gratefully, sinking back into her chair and pulling a bottle out of her bag for Flynn. She cradled his warm little body against hers and he leaned into her, running his fingers over her face as he looked up at her with wide, accusing eyes.

He was still scared. Of course he was, it was going to take time for him to believe that he was safe again. He had been through such a lot in his short life, but Saraya knew, if she could just keep him close, he would be okay. She would be the mother he needed, and he would be able to put his rocky start behind him.

She heard the satisfying sound of the aeroplane door slamming shut and counted the minutes as they ticked slowly by. Looking around she could see plenty of nervous faces. She didn't look out of place in the slightest, though flying was the one thing she *wasn't* afraid of right now. She closed her eyes and waited, listening to the sound of her breath. And at last, the plane began to move.

She opened her eyes to see they were taxiing down

the runway, leaving their troubles far behind. She and Flynn would be together, safe. And never again would they have to be ripped from each other's arms. They would be a proper family. Flynn sighed happily, his eyes sinking closed as he gulped his milk, and finally Saraya let herself burst free with a real smile. They had made it.

Epilogue

"Amelia! Amelia, he's at it again! Make him stop."

Amelia looked up from her book, smiling. "Who's at what again?" she called innocently.

"You *know!*" came the breathless reply.

Amelia laughed. She pushed herself up onto her elbows, folding the corner of her page and placing the book on her blanket. Her feet were caked in sand and her face was hot and sweaty. The tide was rising slowly up the beach, the cool salty water perfect for a pre-dinner dip. She shielded her eyes from the sun and looked over to where the ruckus was coming from, twenty feet up the beach at Mama Jin's little café.

Mama Jin had become entangled in their lives very soon after they had arrived in Cancún in search of a fresh start. Amelia – though back then she had still thought of herself as Saraya – had rented a tiny studio flat from the elderly woman and somehow managed to convince Mama Jin to hire her as a waitress at the small but popular café.

With her powers of persuasion, she had even managed to sweet talk her way into bringing Flynn – or as she had introduced him, Rory – to work with her, where he could roll around on the sand as she served icy cool smoothies to the customers.

Mama Jin had taken the two of them firmly under her wing, accepting their story that she had left an abusive boyfriend behind without question, and offering them her own protection.

Wild haired and brisk mannered with a hard outer shell, it hadn't taken very long for the old Mexican woman to show them another side of her heart. It had been Flynn who had brought that out of her, without a doubt. He had always been able to bring out the best in people, as Amelia knew only too well. Known as Jacinta to everyone else, irritable, wild tempered and fiercely independent, she had quickly shown them her true colours.

She had been a desperately lonely old woman. No children of her own, nobody to love. Widowed at twenty-two, just three years after her marriage to the love of her life, with nothing but a beach-front café to remember her dear husband by. It had made her icy.

But having Amelia and Flynn thrust upon her, had somehow thawed her out. After just a few short months she had become like a grandmother to Rory and a mother to Amelia. Her kindness had made those early days in a strange new world feel a whole lot easier.

"I mean it. This boy is too much!" she cried again. "Come, Amelia, come now!"

Amelia laughed again and stood up, making her way over to the open fronted café. Just inside, sitting on an old warn sofa was Mama Jin, her face red and laughing as a bounding, black haired five year old bounced on her knee. His grin was wide, displaying the gummy space where he had recently lost his first baby tooth.

He looked up at Amelia, their eyes meeting. She felt her heart swell as she watched his joyful expression. "What are you doing, Rory?" she smiled, her eyes crinkling merrily.

"Tickling Mama Jin. Mummy, she's so ticklish,

look!" He jumped down to the floor and picked up a long white feather, stroking it mischievously along the arch of the old woman's dirty bare foot. She squealed and tried to get her feet under the sofa, out of his reach. "See, Mummy?" he giggled.

"I see," she answered, her eyes sparkling. "Now, let's leave this poor woman to catch her breath and go for a swim, shall we?"

Rory jumped up instantly, peeling off his t-shirt and following after Amelia. He grabbed hold of her hand as they walked out of the café, squeezing it in his excitement. He was a natural in the water and Amelia knew he could never resist the lure of a dip. She threw a smile at Mama Jin and received a wink back.

Rory unclasped his fingers from hers and took off across the hot sand. His body no longer had the barrel belly and chunky thighs of a toddler. He had lost the chubby wrists and ankles. Now, he was lithe and brown and she marvelled at how quickly he had grown into the strong, happy boy she loved so very much.

As she watched him bound into the cool waves, she caught herself remembering how intense their beginning had been. How she had been so scared that she would lose him and never get him back. How every single minute with him had been a blessing, because it meant that they were still together and nothing had come between them.

Over the past four and a half years, her life had transformed completely. She no longer felt as though she were filling her time with pointless tasks. She no longer wondered what her purpose was and why life felt so empty. It was hard to believe she'd accepted that bland existence for so long.

Her life was blissfully, wonderfully full now. She'd realised that what she had been searching for was *this*. This deep, unconditional, unbreakable connection. She had given up everything for him, yet she hadn't regretted it even once.

Natalia had once told her that she had saved him. That Flynn would be grateful to her if she ever told him what she had done. How hard she had fought for him as a baby. But Amelia knew differently. It was *he* who had saved her. That tiny black haired, barefoot baby had turned her life upside down. And she would never stop being grateful for that.

The End

About This Story

Writing this book has been a hugely healing process for me. The original idea has been following me around since I was about eight years old. I had been doing a school project about Victorian England, which had affected me deeply. My thoughts were constantly filled with horse-drawn carts, dirty streets, afternoon tea and corsets. I had several memorable dreams during this time, but one stands out above the rest.

In the dream I was a grown woman living in Victorian London. I was walking over a bridge when I heard crying. When I went to investigate under the bridge, there were several filthy children there – all boys, starving, skinny and orphaned. The moment I saw them, I was overcome with an intense need to be their mother. To clean them and feed them, to keep them safe and warm and above all, loved. To give them the childhood they deserved. I have never forgotten that dream.

It wasn't until last year though, that the story of The Promise came together and I knew what I would do with this dream. My second child, a daughter, was born with unexpected and chronic medical issues. We were admitted to the hospital when she was just two days old, and there we would remain for five long months.

It was the most traumatic experience of my life. At eighteen days old, she went for her first surgery. I had been told I would have to hand her to the nurses in the waiting room and not accompany her into the theatre. I had tried to be strong, to hold my emotions together and be the stable, calm presence she deserved. However, as we left the NICU and made our way to the children's theatres, I crumbled.

When we got to the waiting room, I shut down. I put my tiny, sweet baby girl into the sling, held her tight against my chest and focused everything I had on her. I hummed a tune. I kissed her. I rocked.

They came for her. I couldn't do it. I couldn't give them my baby. I just couldn't. I'm sure I looked as if I were on the verge of an epic breakdown. I ignored everyone who came our way. I could hear their voices but I couldn't acknowledge them. I was never going to be ready to peel my hands from my daughter and watch them take her away.

Realising my predicament, they backed down. I was allowed to take her into the theatre. I laid her down softly on the warmed bed. I held her hand and kissed her forehead as they put her to sleep. And then, when my time had run out, I walked away unsure if I would ever see her alive again.

It was the hardest thing I've ever had to do, and that turned out to be the first surgery of many for my sweet baby. Walking away has never gotten any easier.

This experience became the first step to me writing this story. I had to get those feelings of absolute horror and desperation out. This emerged as the scene in which Saraya has been arrested and Flynn is snatched from her arms – my ultimate fear.

With previous books, I have always had an outline of the story, beats to work to. With this one, I had nothing. It came together completely organically, from the depths of my heart and somehow found its way.

What I hope The Promise conveys above all else is a feeling of all consuming, unconditional, unbreakable love between a mother and her child. How we would do anything, even things we never believed possible of ourselves to keep our children safe.

If you enjoyed this story I would be very grateful if you could leave a review on Amazon for me. They make such a huge difference to me as an author and help new readers to find my books.

And if you want to be the first to know about the next book I release, pop over to www.samvickery.com and sign up for my free reader list where you'll get all the latest news and no spam!

Sam Vickery

Also by Sam Vickery

One More Tomorrow

Chapter One

I can't remember a time in my childhood when I ever dreamed of being a mother. Whilst my sisters were cooing over their Tiny Tears dolls, rocking their chubby plastic bodies and jamming magic milk bottles into their oddly triangular mouths, I was in the garden digging a hole to Australia, or climbing up the tall oak tree to launch my teddy from the topmost branches, testing out the latest parachute I'd invented out of a paper napkin and a tangled ball of my mother's wool. I was reading about how planets are formed, or making clay sculptures – which I was sure would make me a famous artist. I was busy, and curious and relentless in my thirst for knowledge. Babies did not interest me in the slightest.

Susie next door had one, a dribbly, demanding six month old brother called Davey – runny gravy, I called him behind her back – who I heard squealing and crying through the thin walls of our terraced house every morning before the sun was even up. I would roll over, huffing and grimacing, pulling my pillow hard over my ears as I tried to block out his piercing intrusions. Babies did not let people sleep, I'd deduced from these frequent unwelcome awakenings.

Susie was a typically proud big sister. She would grin indulgently as he knocked over her carefully constructed tower of bricks, not caring that he was rudely interrupting our game, dragging us out of our imagined world of pirates, magic and adventure to wave a chewed rusk in her face. I hated him.

As I lay in my huge, grown up sized bed now with the pre-dawn haze filtering through the sheer blue curtains, Lucas's warm strong back pressed up against my side as he slept, I wondered if that was why I was being punished. If I had brought on my own misery through some sort of wicked karma. My disdain, or at least my disinterest in babies had carried on right up until I turned twenty-eight. I'd managed to come through school, university, marry Lucas and get a job teaching anthropology – a subject I adored – without ever considering the possibility of motherhood. Lucas had been surprised at my certainty that children were not to be on the cards, but he was willing to box up that dream if it meant keeping me. Everything been just as it should have been. Life was ticking by, following my carefully crafted plan. Everything was perfect. Until my twenty-eighth birthday.

There had been too much vodka for both of us. Laughter, fumbling in the dark, wrapped together in a tangle of limbs and lust. A torn condom that went unnoticed until it was too late. A shared glance of panic and bewilderment in the morning that followed. And then, though I held on to my sense of normal, my orderly, controlled reality, though I grasped onto it with all my might, there was nothing I could do to take back that night. In a few moments of reckless passion everything had changed.

Suddenly, those doors which had been bolted shut, the lock rusted and unmoving, had been burst open with an explosion that shattered them into tiny little splinters. We had done something that could not be undone, and all at once a whole new path lay before us, shining with possibility. And for no reason I could fathom, without reason or logic, I just knew, *I knew* that I had to follow it. As soon as I realised a heart beat other than my own was fluttering inside my womb, depending on me for its very existence, I knew. I was going to be a mother. I wanted it more intensely than I had ever wanted anything. I felt fierce and strong and primal. This was what I was meant to do, I knew it.

Except it wasn't.

Eleven weeks. Eleven precious, wonderful weeks. That's how long I managed to keep him alive. Don't ask me how, but I knew it was a boy. My son. Eleven weeks he grew and developed and changed me in ways that could never be erased. And then, in a wave of crippling cramps and clotted blood, he was gone. My son. My angel.

After he left me, I found I was no longer complete. I was not the person I had been before, I was something new, something empty and lost. I couldn't go back now that I had seen what could be. I couldn't forget how it had felt to be a mother, to be needed so deeply, to love so hard. I couldn't undo it.

Lucas stirred beside me and I glanced through tear fogged eyes at the small silver clock on the bedside cabinet. It had been my mother's and hers before that, and every time I looked at it I remembered with vivid clarity how it had felt to wake up in her big bed as a small child, her tanned arm slung loosely over my torso, the shining silver clock ticking quietly beside us.

She would wake groggy and grumpy, and I would have to cajole her into the day, convince her it really was morning time, though she would groan and refuse to open her eyes. "Just five more minutes, my darling. It's still dark," she would moan from under the covers. I would huff and sigh and fidget impatiently beside her as she ignored me, trying to get a few more precious moments of rest. Then, as if a switch had been flicked on, she would suddenly be ready, throwing the blankets to the ground and grabbing me tight, pulling me in for a hug and kissing me all over my face. I would squeal and try to get away, though really I loved it. She would jump out of bed singing at the top of her voice, her grumpiness forgotten and buried, at least until the next morning. The clock filled me with nostalgia and sadness, yet I refused to part with it. Painful though they were, the memories of my mother were all I had left. They were better than nothing at all.

Lucas stirred again. I wiped my swollen eyes against the pillowcase, though I knew he would know right away that I'd been crying for hours. That my night had been filled with the endless pacing and wicked nightmares I was fast becoming used to. He always wanted to talk, to get me to tell him every little detail of what was upsetting me. To share the horror of the nightmares, the stories I told myself in the dark quiet hours. It was pointless. He knew that as well as I did, but he kept on trying, pushing, wanting to be there for me, to fix everything. But I couldn't be fixed. He knew that too.

Sometimes Lucas would wake in those dark, lonely hours, despite my tooth-marked fist, my swallowed, muffled sobs. When he found me in such a state, he would look at me with those big brown eyes glistening in the moonlight with tears he wouldn't shed, his mouth pursed in indecision and sadness. He would take me in his arms and hold me tight until I pretended to fall back to sleep. His comfort never helped. I didn't deserve it. I wanted to suffer alone. I didn't want to see the look of anguish in his eyes.

On this occasion though, I had managed to get a hold of myself before he woke. He would know I'd been crying again, of course. He could always tell. But I wouldn't flaunt it. I never did. Perhaps this morning we could pretend it hadn't happened. I didn't have it in me to talk about it again. At least not yet.

I felt the feather-light touch of his fingertips as they grazed their way through my hair, making their way down my spine. I shivered, instinctively leaning into the security of his warmth. "Good morning," he said, his throat raspy with the after effects of sleep as he nuzzled into my neck.

"Good morning yourself," I replied, my voice falsely bright as I turned to face my husband. He pursed his full lips into a scowl as he caught sight of my puffy eyes and blotchy cheeks, his thick, dark brows furrowing. Even so, I thought, he was still indisputably good looking. His cheekbones were defined and strong. His eyelashes thick, his eyes a pool of rich chocolate. And under the thin sheets, I could make out the defined muscles of his chest and shoulders.

He was a big man at six and a half feet tall. Being only five feet and two measly inches myself, I had always liked that about him. I used to love it when he wrapped me in those massive arms, and made me feel like nothing could hurt me. These days, though, even he couldn't protect me from my pain.

"Rox…" he began, his voice deep and serious. I shook my head.

"Don't, Lucas. Don't. Not today." He twisted his lips again and gave me a long, stern look. Indecision flickered in his eyes. He gave a quick nod and pulled me wordlessly into his chest. I felt myself tense against him as he kissed the top of my head and sighed. Fearing his kindness would only make me start sobbing all over again, I cleared my throat and pulled away, hopping out of bed without meeting his eyes. I could feel his stare burning into my back. I wrapped my cotton dressing gown around my shivering body, pulling my thick dark hair out from under the collar as I headed for the bathroom. "Don't forget, we've got my sisters coming over for lunch today," I told him over my shoulder.

"As if I would forget a visit from the Cormack family," Lucas said, smiling, though it didn't meet his eyes. I paused by the bedroom door, looking at a framed photograph on the wall of my family from last summer. It made me smile every time I saw it, though I never failed to notice the empty space where my mother should have been. My younger sisters, Isabel and Bonnie were identical twins, yet their personalities could not have been more different. Isabel was introverted, sweet, and bordering on genius. We'd expected her to become a physicist, a computer programmer, an entrepreneur, or something equally brilliant and fitting to her intelligence. Yet, she'd surprised us all by choosing to go into social work. She'd actually turned down several promotions because they meant moving away from the personal, one on one duties with the families and children she worked with, to go and push papers around an office instead. Isabel had explained that no pay rise in the world would be enough to pull her away from the people who needed her most. I suspected she thrived on the drama and excitement. Isabel was at her absolute best in a crisis. She was down to earth despite her brilliance, and barely a day went by without us seeing one another.

Bonnie had a polar opposite character to Isabel. Her personality was nothing short of extreme. She was loud, flakey and possibly the most honest person I had ever known. She would say whatever she thought, no matter the consequences. Lucas had once told her she had no filter, to which she'd told him filters were for shifty people and at least he knew what she really thought of him. Thankfully, I had been informed, she liked him. A couple of her exes had not got off nearly so lightly. Though she could be wild and unpredictable, Bonnie was also the most empathetic person I had ever known. She could see right through pretence, right to the source of the pain. A skill she used often, and which proved more than a little annoying when I was trying to pretend I was fine, thank you very much!

As sisters, and as friends we were as close as it gets. Our father had passed away from cancer when the twins were just two. I had been four. And then, we had lost our mother fourteen years later. Now it was just the three of us left from our little family, and the losses had created an unbreakable bond between us. I turned from the photograph, facing Lucas now, and gave him a genuine smile, not the false happy mask I had been pasting on all week. "I know you would never forget," I said. "Thank you." He nodded as he watched me pick up my wash-bag and walk into the bathroom. I could feel his pitying stare burning into my back.

One More Tomorrow is Available on Kindle and Paperback now.

26461016R00154

Printed in Great Britain
by Amazon